# The air quivered

The tarmac became a battlefield as Gunter Dykstra turned to see his old friend emerge from the hangar. But the Dutchman's smile of greeting was transformed into a rictus of shock when he saw the Browning.

It was aimed directly at him.

Nile Barrabas fired.

Two shots resounded across the open space. Gunter stared at his friend. Their eyes met, milliseconds before the Dutchman's face exploded into a red death mask. He stumbled backward, throwing his hands in the air before falling against the wheels of the airplane.

Barrabas reeled from the sight. He made an effort to run, but without warning a steel club slammed against the back of his skull. All sensation drained from his body. Barrabas felt himself suspended on the precipice of a great void as he collapsed into the darkness of nonexistence.

# SOBs
## SOLDIERS OF BARRABAS

# SOBs
### SOLDIERS OF BARRABAS

# *POINT BLANK*

## *JACK HILD*

## A GOLD EAGLE BOOK FROM
# W🌐RLDWIDE

TORONTO • NEW YORK • LONDON • PARIS
AMSTERDAM • STOCKHOLM • HAMBURG
ATHENS • MILAN • TOKYO • SYDNEY

First edition March 1987

ISBN 0-373-61617-1

Special thanks and acknowledgment to
Robin Hardy for his contribution to this work.

Printed in Canada

**1**

He awakened, pounding his fist into the pillow, driven by an inhuman panic bordering on fury. He stopped, felt himself lathered in a cold sweat and rolled over. Frozen with rage, he stared for a few moments at the ceiling of the Cairo hotel room. It was already midnight.

The lights from the teeming city flickered across his scarred body when he pushed himself from the bed. He threw open the glass doors to the balcony and was assaulted by a pounding wave of smells and noise from the frantic traffic, carried by the dusty dry winds blowing in from the Western Desert.

The angular modern lines of the fabled city were pierced by shafts of minarets and domed mosques with their soft feminine curves. The Nile, the ancient river whose name he bore, was a dark cut through Cairo's center. With ancient dignity, it wound north on the final stretch of the relentless journey that took it four thousand miles from Africa's jungle heart to the Mediterranean.

Nile Barrabas brushed his hand slowly through his white crew cut hair in a gesture of bewilderment and stepped outside into Cairo's dusty purple night.

It was the war. It came back to him like some distant echo, trapped for years in the barren canyons of painful memory, building to a deafening roar that threatened to engulf him. He gripped the railing of the balcony and leaned forward. Vietnam. Erika. Heiss. Ghosts from a dead past had gathered for some mysterious reason in the land of pharaohs. Why here? Why now? It was midnight. Time to go.

The nightmare flashed behind his eyes again with unexpected vividness. He knew it had happened in Quang Doc, and that he had been young then, but the month, the year and the reason were blurred by the generous mists of time. The Vietcong force had ambushed his patrol, knocking out the point and the tail, closing in on all sides and cutting them down.

It happened so quickly—or perhaps it only seemed quick to a bunch of green soldiers—that the will to live was an adrenaline surge inside them. They fought back. Seven of them were still alive, still primed to kill, when it was over. Seventeen VC and seven of their buddies were piled knee-high in a circle of gore. Covered in blood, the survivors were unable to speak, to cry or to feel. No one knew how long it had taken. In the aftermath a single image remained, burned into Barrabas's mind.

It was the moment his M-16 jammed.

A VC, bayonet raised, stumbled slightly as he came at Barrabas. He tried to recover, and did, but too late. The split-second error gave it to the Special Forces captain. Barrabas took his useless rifle by the barrel, the red-hot metal burning into his hands unnoticed. For a moment, a flicker of time so brief he might have imagined it, his blue eyes met the liquid-brown ellipses of the Asian's.

If I hadn't slipped, I would be killing you, the Vietnamese said with his eyes. If there had been no war, we might have been friends. In that moment Barrabas wondered if fate was willful or just indifferent. It was a question he never answered.

He slammed the butt of his rifle into the Cong's head, dropping him instantly, destroying his face. Then he raised his gun again and swung a second time and a third; he kept swinging, pounding blood, bone and brain matter into the porous brown earth until there was nothing left.

Now, when he dreamed it, the rifle butt was raised, there was realization in the Asian eyes, but when the butt hit, it became his arm, and the Asian vanished, transformed into Erika. He was slamming his fists into her face, and she was screaming for him to stop.

He shuddered as the cold afterimage of the dream filtered through his waking consciousness, throwing his head back and gasping for air. A groan rasped from his open mouth, like a scream he had strangled deep in his throat. Desert winds, hot despite the night, brushed against his skin, tickling and teasing, a merciless reminder of life. Would it have come to that, he wondered, if Erika hadn't left me first? The question frightened him. But he knew the answer. Something was happening to him, and she had seen it coming.

It was Heiss, he told himself. Karl Heiss had returned from the dead, and with him the memory of what he had done to Erika, of what he had done in Vietnam. It was midnight. Time to go.

The waters of the Nile danced with the lights of busy Cairo. If troubles were a river, could they be followed to their source? The river drew him; the gaze it returned to him was passive, benign.

It had been so for fifty centuries.

It would be so for fifty more.

BARRABAS GRIPPED the handle above the window in the back seat of the battered taxi as the driver tore recklessly through the narrow stone streets of Bab al-Khalq, skirting the edge of Cairo's Old City, where the medieval streets were too narrow for twentieth-century vehicles. There would be no element of surprise. The taxi's manifold had been crushed when the engine had collapsed on worn-out mounts. The explosive racket of internal combustion echoed off the facades of the brick and stucco houses lining the street. The American mercenary could barely hear his thoughts.The driver slowed slightly as they passed the mighty stone ramparts of the forbidding citadel built by Saladin, the Islamic warrior who had swept the Crusaders from Africa and most of Palestine eight hundred years earlier. He pushed himself close to the windshield, peering through the layers of dust at the fork in the road ahead. He chose the road on the left. Tires squealed in protest, and the taxi lurched up the slope of the Muqattam Hills.

Cairo spread across the Nile Valley, lights glinting and twinkling through the dusty air as far as the eye could see. At the foot of the hills, the darkness was broken by scattered lights from squatters' fires. The glowing yellow dome of the city cast into relief long straight streets lined with perfectly square stone houses. These were the houses of the dead, the tombs of the Southern Cemetery, one of the great necropolises at the edge of Cairo, which rivaled in size entire quarters of the Egyptian city.

Abruptly, where the night had grown darker, the taxi halted. The pandemonium of the overcrowded capital had been left behind; now the sound of insects, strange rustlings and distant growls, and the foul stench of rot and pig shit, launched another, more stealthy assault.

"Zabalin!" the driver spat with contempt through his open window. "The People of the Garbage. You go here now? You crazee man."

The Zabalin were the garbage-pickers of Cairo, forty thousand strong. In the city of fourteen million people, municipal services had been completely disrupted by revolution, war and overcrowding. Only remarkable tenacity enabled the peasants who streamed into the urban mecca to survive, and the Zabalin had carved a niche for themselves by loading thousands of tons of the city's garbage into donkey carts and removing it to the dumps on the outskirts each day. They lived here, too, with their families, in improvised shanties or on streets carved from piles of rubbish two stories high.

Everything was recycled and sold for a pittance to the cottage industries of Cairo. By day Zabalin wives and children sorted junk, separating into enormous piles as long as city blocks bits of broken glass, scrap metal, carbon from old batteries, clothing to make rags and rinds and slops to feed dirty disease-ridden pigs. The Zabalin were indispensable to Cairo's existence. For this they were despised.

Barrabas squeezed off several Egyptian pounds from the roll he carried in the breast pocket of his cotton khaki shirt and thrust them at the driver.

"That's for the ride. And to forget."

The driver's eyes lit up at the sight of the generous tip. He couldn't care less about the American's choice of neighborhood. The money vanished inside his shirt. Money killed memory, and only money would revive it.

"I wait!" He nodded with an eager smile. His teeth shone with saliva. The smell of cash apparently overwhelmed the stench of the Zabalin.

"No." Barrabas shook his head. "You go." He opened the door and got out.

"I wait!" The driver was either persistent or didn't understand English.

Barrabas flipped another Egyptian pound through the front window into his lap.

"You go." He jerked his thumb over his shoulder in the direction of Cairo.

The taxi rumbled away, the earsplitting noise of the muffler fading slowly as the car lurched and staggered back down the Muqattam Hills. Barely had Barrabas been left in silence when an Arab emerged from the night and stood before him. He wore a suit jacket and vest over his blue-striped djellaba, the traditional Egyptian garb that resembled an old-fashioned nightgown. His dark hair was wrapped in a dirty cloth, a scavenger's disheveled version of a turban. He gave Barrabas a toothy smile and bowed deeply in greeting.

"Sharif al-Hakim," he introduced himself in flawless English. He had a short, carefully combed beard, a scraggly mustache and apple-red cheeks against olive skin. His blue eyes glistened in the dim cast-off light from the nearby city. They were eyes that could be trusted. But the solid feel of the Browning HP strapped under the American's shirt was reassuring.

"Barrabas."

"Yes. I know. I recognize you. The description I was given is accurate. You also have a Browning under your left arm."

The white-haired merc shrugged. The Arab obviously wasn't disturbed by it.

"It is perfectly safe here," al-Hakim said, gesturing toward the city of garbage that lay heaped around them. "No one comes except the Zabalin—and, of course, some inept government bureaucrats, or from time to time an obscure Canadian journalist concerned about the plight of the Third World. But never at night. At night there are the fleshpots of Giza to attend to."

"I was told you had some news. That Heiss is back."

The Arab's confidence in the safety of their surroundings seemed to disappear. Edgy, he put his arms up to stop Barrabas from talking.

"Softly! Such that even the jinni do not hear," al-Hakim whispered, referring to the supernatural spirits of Arab lore.

"What do you know?"

"It is not I who knows. It is a Nubian merchant, a man named Atbar, who brought the information. This man you seek, he is in Africa."

Barrabas tensed, his breath coming in short excited stabs. "Africa is a big place."

"But I understand too small a continent for two such enemies as you."

"Too small a planet. You're certain it's Heiss?"

"That is the name this white man has used. He bought supplies from the caravans that cross the Sudan and had them taken on foot deep into the equatorial jungles. He has suffered a terrible wound, I am told. A recent one. It has deformed him in some way. He is almost always in pain. Is this the man you seek?"

Barrabas shrugged, shaking his head slowly. "I haven't seen him eyeball to eyeball in a long time, Sharif. What did he buy from this Nubian merchant?"

"Weapons?" Al-Hakim put his hands out in a gesture of ignorance. "Slaves? Atbar has an extraordinary talent for meeting the obscure desires of his customers."

"If his information is accurate, he'll lose a customer. Why is he willing to talk to me?"

Sharif al-Hakim's blue eyes glinted as he raised his brows. "Like most Nubians, Atbar is superstitious. This man will kill without a moment's thought. Atbar believes a devil lives inside his honored customer, but he is too frightened to destroy the devil himself. But come, he is waiting to speak to you. And for the money."

"Where?"

"Deeper," he said, pointing with a flashlight to the streets of cardboard shanties that burrowed through the detritus of Cairo. The mud road was strewn with filth and riddled with fetid dark puddles. It curved along the side of a mountain chain of rags, the peaks towering several stories high. The Arab and the American passed rows of crooked shacks, where the Zabalin had carefully woven cardboard, corrugated tin and bits of precious wood into shelters. A black sow trotted past them, followed by her five piglets, which stopped to forage at the garbage along the road.

Barrabas turned in response to the creepy shudder that crawled up the back of his neck. A pack of six wild dogs trotted warily only a few feet behind them. They were emaciated, and their fur was dirty and splotched by disease. Their eyes were lit by hunger. The lead dog stopped and growled, revealing sharp yellow teeth and bleeding gums.

"Do not look back," the Arab whispered, tugging at the American's sleeve. "They will go away. If they do not, you will need your gun after all."

Almost simultaneously, men and dogs entered a small clearing among the hills of garbage, where paths snaked off in several directions. The sow and her piglets were rooting in the slops near the body of a dead donkey. The dogs rushed forward, growling, their bared teeth ripping through the night. They crowded around the decaying carcass, tearing at the rotten flesh and snapping at one another.

"This way," al-Hakim urged, pointing the flashlight. "The Nubian is waiting." He led Barrabas deeper into the gruesome warren.The rank odor of the dump thickened, weighting the air, and Barrabas fought the natural reaction of his stomach. They left the mountains of rags and wandered among rolling, tangled hills of broken metal past shelters created from hubcaps or the hoods and trunks of wrecked cars. He knew that Zabalin eyes followed them carefully through cracks in the rough shanty walls.

Once again the narrow muddy road opened into a clearing. The mounds of metal rubbish ended in a precipice on one side. On the other, grunting noises and the soft thud of many hooves indicated a field of pigpens. The smell of excrement was almost unbearable. Sharif al-Hakim's face clouded in surprise and alarm as he looked around.

''He is go—''

The sound of a razor slashing the wind stole the Egyptian's words. Barrabas dropped, rolling backward through the mud and filth as his hand reached through the open buttons of his shirt and gripped the handle of his Browning. Light glinted briefly on the sharp metal blade of a long machete, swinging from the hands of a Nubian giant.

The terrible knife cut through al-Hakim's neck as if it were soft butter, and his head flew from the stump. The decapitated torso blew a geyser of dark liquid high in the air before the body dropped like a bundle of dirty rags. There were angry grunts and the trampling of hooves as the Egyptian's head sailed into the pigpen.Barrabas pulled his gun free and twisted to face their attacker. The Nubian moved forward with giant strides, the long machete raised, blood frenzy written across his eager face. Suddenly he stopped. The expression on his face changed. He turned stiffly to look behind him.

Barrabas swung the gun around, his finger pressing the trigger. A man—no, a boy—stood in the darkness of the rubbish heap, his blue-and-white striped djellaba billowing forward in the fine breezes. His face and clothing were streaked with dirt, his arm outstretched, shoulder forward. The Nubian crumpled like a slashed tire and fell on top of al-Hakim's headless body. The handle of a long knife protruded from his back. Not far away, in the maze of streets that ran through the foul mountains of garbage, the growls of the wild dogs answered the clarion call of fresh blood.

Barrabas pushed himself up from the muck, sick to his stomach, his clothing awash in slimy ordure.

The Zabalin looked at him, his bright eyes flicking quickly from the gun in the American's hand to his face. He walked forward, apparently unafraid. Planting one foot firmly on the dead Nubian's broad back, he pulled the knife out with both hands and wiped it on his djellaba.

The pack of wild dogs burst around the corner of one of the roads and leaped frantically for the corpses sprawled in the mud, tearing at them and fighting over the meat. Beyond them, the young man held his long knife up in a gesture of victory. Barrabas met his eyes in silent gratitude.

The Zabalin nodded once and melted into the Egyptian night.

THE ANTIQUE ORMOLU CLOCK on the marble fire-place struck midnight as Gunter arrived. Erika Dyk-stra stepped smoothly across the living room of the seventeenth-century Amsterdam townhouse, her stocking feet sinking into the pile of the Persian carpet. She stopped by the wall-sized mirror in the foyer, quickly adjusting the folds of her light blue dress, and brushed her blond hair over her shoulders. She double-checked the makeup around her eyes. Her visitor wouldn't notice that she had been crying unless he looked very closely. To make sure, she turned the dimmer switch, lowering the level of light. The bell chimed again, twice, persistently. She opened the door.

"Little sister! I came as soon as I could."

Erika almost disappeared into her brother's burly arms as he embraced and pulled her to him. As he let go, he peered more closely at her face.

"You have been crying! Why have you been crying?"

She looked at him, shaking her head to deny it, but her lower lip quivered, and suddenly against her will the dam broke, streaking her face with tears.

"Come!" For the second time, Gunter took her in his arms and hugged her. They stood that way for several minutes until he felt the sobs that racked her body stop.

"Oh, Gunter." She turned slowly into the living room. "I'm sorry I'm such a pain. It's just—"

"You're no pain!" Gunter said in a loud and reassuring voice. "It's what we've always done for each other. So. You received a letter from him? What kind of letter?''

''From his lawyer in Zurich. It's here.'' Erika lifted a thick white envelope from a small table and handed it to Gunter. ''I can't believe it's him. I just can't believe it.''

Erika sniffed delicately and sat in a chair by the cold fireplace as her brother began to read. She had met Nile Barrabas in Vietnam during the war. Her private business, an import-export firm, had specialized in smuggling. Rich Vietnamese paid well to have their gold and antiques taken from the country before the inevitable fall. Occasionally, with Gunter, she had given the CIA some assistance, taking agents and messages deep inside enemy territory on company airplanes.

She and her brother had already made their first million when she'd met the young major on relief on a beach north of Saigon. They'd disappeared to a hotel for the weekend and had fallen in love. That had been a long time ago. Still, she could not believe that it had come to this.

Gunter finished the letter from Barrabas's lawyer and riffled through the supplementary pages that had been attached.

''One pearl necklace. Ten emeralds, five raw and five cut. A three-carat ruby. Two Sevres vases, eighteenth century. Two paintings, the Matisse and a Chagall?'' He looked up at her. ''I didn't know you had a Chagall.''

Erika shrugged. "It's upstairs in the bedroom. Chagalls were cheap last year. Paris was full of them. That's where he bought it."

"And now he wants it all back."

She nodded. "It's a complete list of everything he ever gave me. According to Herr Heinzmuller, the eminent Swiss attorney, they were merely in my custody for safekeeping. Can you believe that? He bought a pearl necklace for himself and left it here just...just for the hell of it!"

She was breathing hard, and sparks of anger flew from her eyes. "And if these things aren't returned in a week, I'm to reimburse him to the tune of 2.3 million dollars or face a Swiss court."

Gunter made a grimace and threw himself onto an overstuffed chesterfield. He waved one hand in the air as he spoke and shoved the letter onto a table.

"Erika, my sister. If you are so attached to these trinkets, it is a simple matter for us to forward a bank draft in the amount he requests, and that will be the end of it. However, in the circumstances, I don't think..."

He paused, looking at the beautiful woman he had taken care of since she was nine and he fourteen. "I would think you would not want to be reminded of the circumstances and might be better rid of these objects."

She gave him a long, stony look, scarcely believing what she'd heard.

"I will personally take them to Zurich," Gunter added generously, "and pick you up another Chagall, a bigger one, in Paris on the way home."

Erika's face flushed. She was livid with anger. "Gunter. Do you know what you are saying?" She spoke in a low, even voice. "I don't give a bloody damn about the Chagall, the emeralds, none of it!"

She grabbed the letter from the table and hurled it at him. It fluttered and fell onto the carpet. Suddenly her restraint cracked and her voice faltered. "Don't you understand? I'm worried, Gunter. About Nile." She burst into tears. "All I really care about is him!"

The beautiful Dutch woman buried her face in the back of the chair and sobbed hopelessly. Gunter's head turned from the discarded letter to his baby sister and back to the letter. He felt ashamed. He had assumed terrible things—the worst—about his sister. And about his old friend, Nile Barrabas, as well.

Gunter pushed himself up from the thick cushions and kneeled before the crying woman. He put his thick arm around her slender shoulders and stroked her hair.

"I'm sorry, Erika. I spoke like a selfish man, thinking only of myself. You see, you were the one who said no to Nile Barrabas. You turned him away, and in some ways that can wound a man more than a bullet or the blade of a knife. No. No, you are right. There is something very strange here. Nile Barrabas is a gentleman. He would never do this. Never. There has been a mistake."

Erika steeled herself, pulling herself together and wiping her eyes. Gunter moved back slowly to the couch, maintaining a grip on her hand. She pulled away from him, stood and walked stiffly to the fireplace. Staring at the ormolu clock, she wrung her hands nervously.

"That's just it, Gunter. Maybe there wasn't a mistake. He's changed. I could feel it. Something inside him was different. It was after Heiss took me as a hostage in order to lure him to his death. I . . . I was afraid of him after that, of everything about him, of his experiences in Vietnam, of all the private mercenary armies he's fought in since then. I don't know why."

She faced Gunter squarely. "I was suddenly afraid of his entire life, of everything he had done, of who and what he was. So maybe there isn't a mistake, Gunter. Don't you see? That's the worst of it. I don't even know for sure. I don't...I don't ..." She was on the edge of tears again, and her voice broke. Her brother walked to the fireplace and stood beside her. He clutched her hands in his to stop her from wringing them. It was through his sister that he had met Nile Barrabas, and the two men had become buddies, sharing booze and the occasional bamboozle on more than a few of the professional soldier's assignments. They were close, but not as close as Barrabas and Erika had been.

He couldn't say for sure that Erika was right about Barrabas. But he knew one thing. Erika had changed, too. Since that episode with Heiss, she had never been the same. She was too easily startled, and the cool, even disposition which had made her one of the wealthiest women in Holland had given way to a quick temper and volatile emotions.

The blame, he suspected, lay both ways. In matters of love, that was serious damage. Only the gods knew if it could ever be put back to what it had been. And in Gunter's experience the gods, who doled out pleasures as if there were no tomorrow, were misers in matters of love.

"I will go to see him," Gunter announced, pounding his fist against his massive chest. He grabbed the attorney's letter from the carpet and waved it at Erika. She looked at him as if he were crazy.

"You can't mean it. What good will you do?"

He shook his head with a look of absolute certainty. "There has been a mistake. I will see him. We will talk."

"But it's impossible. He's in Cairo."

"You know this?" Gunter looked at her skeptically. Erika's protest was too tentative to be meant. He knew when he was being manipulated by his sister.

Erika looked embarrassed. "I phoned Walker Jessup in New York. It's his job to know where Nile is."

"And he told you this!"

A little smile flickered on the beautiful Dutch woman's face. "Remember the caviar we just got out of Russia? From the Lake Baikal sturgeon?"

Gunter nodded, a sinking feeling in his stomach. The sturgeons' eggs were a rare delicacy, worth a fortune in the West. He'd gone through hell finding an airplane to smuggle the Rolls-Royce to the Kremlin bureaucrat who had arranged the deal.

"I traded it for the information."

"All of it?"

Erika nodded reluctantly.

Gunter roared. "There was more caviar there than any man could eat in a lifetime!"

"Even Walker Jessup?"

Gunter closed his eyes and winced. Then he nodded slowly. "Maybe Walker Jessup," he admitted. "Oh, Erika, couldn't you have saved half of it? A quarter?"

The blonde leaned forward, standing on tiptoes to kiss her big brother's lips. "Oh, Gunter, will you go to Cairo? Just to see if he's all right." She leaned against his chest, murmuring the words like a prayer. "Just make sure he's all right."

Gunter squeezed her tightly. He picked her up off the floor and swung her through the air, much as he had done when they were children.

Erika shrieked in surprise, breaking forth in a smile of relief. *"Dank u wel, mijn broer. Dank u wel!"*

"For my beautiful little sister, it is nothing. I go to Cairo and see this man who means so much to you. *Ja, ja,*" he said, laughing as he set her down. He nodded and threw his arms sideways into the air, mocking defeat as he headed for the door. "How the Americans say it? I know when I am beat."

## 2

As long as he lived, Barrabas would not forget the look on the face of the desk manager when he returned to the luxury hotel in downtown Cairo.

"Any messages?" Barrabas asked, chin up and apparently oblivious to the filth covering his clothes. Well-dressed tourists cast him odd looks and moved away, their noses crinkling in disgust from the pungent odor.

"None this evening, sir," the dignified hotelier replied with the usual deference. If guests had the connections and the money necessary to register there, they had every right to walk through the lobby streaked in mud, excrement or, as far as he was concerned, tar and feathers. Indeed, some of his less fortunate guests had done exactly that during the revolution in 1952—albeit against their will. He rang a little brass bell looped between his third and fourth finger and waved to a young Arab porter.

"Fetch a bottle of Scotch from the bar and deliver it to Mr. Barrabas's room, on the double," the manager instructed. He turned back to the American. "Compliments of the hotel, sir."

Barrabas saluted. Discrete managers earned substantial tips. "And a car and driver in fifteen minutes."

"May I enquire as to the destination and distance, sir?"

"Giza. The nightclub strip. Near the Pyramids."

In his room he showered quickly, tossing back several jiggers of the good Scotch to clear the smell from his nose and throat. The Arab porter reappeared at the door as Barrabas finished dressing. He held a big white laundry bag.

"You had something for the cleaners, sir."

Barrabas smiled inwardly. In expensive hotels, guests paid to have the oddest forms of behavior treated as commonplace. Rich people were eccentric. Poor people could only afford to be crazy. As a recent American president had put it, life is unfair. He lifted his soiled clothing gingerly by two fingers and dropped it into the bag.

A few minutes later, his newest driver made a suicide run through a phalanx of cars circling Tahrir Square, almost climbing the neoclassical steps of the colonnaded Egyptian Museum to avoid a caravan of tourist buses. Somehow they made it to the bridge that crossed Gezirah Island, leading to the western bank of the Nile. Soon, they left behind the tangled streets, thick with high rises, and coasted south on the road to Giza.

Cairo's garish western-style nightclub strip had grown up between the tourist hotels on the highway leading to the Pyramids twenty miles south of the city. Honky-tonk lights in Arab script blinked and flickered in full view of the five thousand year old monuments to the glory of dead kings. A few months earlier Shiite fundamentalists—the extremist Islamic sect that had already taken over Iran and assassinated one Egyptian president—had rioted and run amok among the bars and discos. Many of the buildings were now dark, their facades blackened from smoke and flames, their windows and doors hastily bricked up.

"Here," Barrabas announced to the driver as they approached the brightly lit parking lot outside a hotel resort. A giant neon sign spelled out The Sahara Club.

The Sahara was so notorious that the fun-hating Shiites saw it as a symbol of Western decadence, a bastion of belly dancing and mixed drinks. When the frenzied mob had turned up at its doors, brandishing torches, they had encountered a cordon of tight-lipped employees holding submachine guns. The Shiites had wisely regrouped and moved several blocks down the street where they had burned out the cocktail lounge in the atrium of the Pyramid Vacation Inn.

Barrabas left the taxi and entered the resort complex tossing a curt nod at the colossal doorman, who recognized him from his visit earlier that day. He followed the twisting, discordant sound of Eastern music inside.

The lounge was long, low-ceilinged and decorated like the ersatz harem quarters of an Arabian palace. The air was thick with tobacco smoke and the smell of hashish. A woman dressed in a green bikini with spangles and gold bands about her wrists and neck, writhed and undulated her naked belly on a stage at the far end of the room. Men pointed and clapped.

She leaned low over the front tables, jiggling her breasts tantalizingly before their noses. The brave and the drunk thrust paper currency into her cleavage, and she pulled back with a twist, her tongue darting in saucy defiance.

Barrabas took a seat near the door. Assorted informers, betrayers and representatives of most of the world's infamous secret service agencies took up space at many of the tables. The Israeli Mossad had a table next to South Africa's Bureau of State Security, and across the room a CIA agent sat with agents of the Chilean secret police and operatives from West Germany. Three dour men in ill-cut dark suits nearby were obviously KGB.

Next to booze and hashish, the most valuable and sought-after commodity here was information, and it always went to the highest bidder. The man Barrabas sought was not there yet. But the stint Barrabas had done years earlier in military intelligence for Uncle Sam had taught him that in the underground patience was, if not its own reward, man's greatest virtue. He ordered a Scotch and waited.

As he sipped the fiery liquid, he drifted back for a moment to Vietnam when he was a young army major in MAC and Karl Heiss was an uncooperative CIA agent. In the course of his intelligence work, he had uncovered Heiss's heroin-smuggling operation. It was not just a matter of liquid death. Heiss did not just kill the users; he threw away the lives of young American soldiers to ensure his profits made their way through VC lines.

Karl Heiss wasn't the only bad man in the world who had an appetite for big bucks. But Barrabas had a theory about him. Heiss didn't care about the money; he cared about the kill. The money was only a means and an excuse.

After Nam their paths had crossed a half-dozen times in the decade of mercenary wars Nile Barrabas had gone on to fight, and again, after Walker Jessup had organized the SOBs as a covert-action team on classified assignment for the secret House Committee in Washington.

Once, Barrabas swore he saw Heiss's dead body in the back alley of a Moroccan city, blood dribbling from more holes than he could count. A year later Heiss was at it again, in collusion with Kolubban terrorists to supplant an infant African democracy. Barrabas had left him on the airport runway to rot in a Kolubban jail.

Now he wished he'd pulled the trigger then and there and gotten the bloody thing over with. Because what happened next he could never forget. Heiss had vowed to destroy Barrabas, and to get to him he had kidnapped Erika Dykstra and held her prisoner. Had Barrabas not gotten there first, he would have raped her as well. And somehow, once again, Heiss had gotten away.

The man had friends in high places. The CIA wanted him around for bizarre reasons of their own. But there were others, too, powerful shadowy figures who controlled many resources and who paid the renegade agent to do their dirty work. That was the mystery surrounding Karl Heiss that Barrabas wanted solved. But first he wanted to get Heiss for what the man had done to him and Erika. He wanted Heiss dead. Hacked up, bottled and labeled in some forensics lab or cremated. Dead forever.

A retired U.S. Army colonel with a background in military intelligence, Barrabas had a few resources of his own. After the debacle with Erika in Sri Lanka, he'd quietly put out the word that any news of Heiss was to be relayed to him. They had skirmished in Ethiopia but once again Heiss had disappeared, his fate unknown. A year later, the message had come. Heiss was alive. Someone had seen him, and Nile Barrabas had gone to Cairo.

Now he knew something else was going on—some strange, quiet manipulation that had led him to an Egyptian garbage dump for a midnight rendezvous with Atbar, the mad Nubian, and his singing machete. There was only one thing worse than pig shit: the stench of Heiss at work. Right now, it smelled bad all over.

His man came in the door of the Sahara Club lounge.

Al Ratchett had been MI5 twenty years earlier when the British still thought they had interests in North Africa worth spying for. He was so successful that London had kept him in the field. By the time they were ready to bring him back, it was too late. He had gone native. He became a casualty of the espionage wilderness, forced into exile by his masters and abandoned there.

Now he lived on a miserly pension whose value sank in step with the British economy. He picked up a few bucks here and there for tidbits of useful information he could sell and anesthetized himself to the whole experience with booze and hashish. Still, the climate seemed to agree with him. His tanned, leathery face looked ten years younger than his forty-five years, and he invariably sported a friendly smile. Like the venerable colonialists of a bygone era, the tall, thin man wore a white tropical suit, liberally streaked with the Cairene dust that blew perpetually across the city from the Western Desert.

Barrabas waved to him, and the Brit acknowledged it with a careful toss of his head. He turned to a young woman, neatly dressed in a crisp safari suit, and spoke to her. She nodded in agreement and disappeared into the lobby. Ratchett moved toward Barrabas's table, his eyes slowly scanning the room.

"Good to see you, old chap!" He reached for a chair, carefully pulling his pant legs up at the knees as he sat. Again he looked around in the immediate vicinity of the table to see who was within listening distance.

"They're oil workers," Barrabas told him, referring to a nearby table. A group of European men toasted one another's bad jokes and yelled unseductive invitations at the belly dancer across the lounge. The KGB table was eyeing them with considerable interest. Ratchett leaned his elbow on the table and rested his cheek casually in his hand, shielding his mouth as he spoke.

"Lipreading is a standard part of every KGB agent's prep school training these days, I understand. Al-Hakim gave you what you wanted?"

Barrabas shook his head. "There was a little altercation. Al-Hakim lost his head."

Ratchett looked at him, for a moment misunderstanding. Suddenly comprehension flashed in his eyes. "No! Not really!"

Barrabas nodded once and took another sip of his Scotch. "The Nubian had a knife. Actually a machete. He's no longer a problem."

Ratchett leaned back in his chair and signaled the waiter to bring a round of the same.

"Bit of a sticky wicket, was it?" he mused. "I apologize sincerely, Nile, for peddling you the bait to that trap, whatever it was. Poor al-Hakim. He was a useful informant. Now I shall have to visit his widow and children."

"Who set the trap? Any ideas?"

The former British agent eyeballed a fat KGB operative who was watching them. The Russian returned the stare and phlegmatically turned away. Ratchett leaned forward on his elbow, again shielding his mouth with his hand.

"So far, you know as much as I do. Heiss's name is on a list, a sort of private-missing persons list, if you will. You aren't the only person with a vendetta, Nile. I've confided this list to my informants. Sharif told me a man from the Sudan had information about Karl Heiss. That's when I got hold of you. You learned nothing?"

"Two things that al-Hakim said on the way to the rendezvous. That Heiss was somewhere in equatorial Africa. And that somehow he'd been terribly wounded. That's—" Barrabas stopped when he saw the look of surprise that crossed Ratchett's face. The former British agent squeezed his eyes together and wiped his hand across his face, a gesture of fatigue. The waiter arrived and set two glasses of whiskey on the table. Ratchett looked grim, and stood abruptly.

He paid the waiter. "Bring a third," he instructed, then faced Barrabas. "Wait here, old chap. No promises, but it might be your lucky day."

A few moments later he reappeared with the neatly dressed young woman in tow. She was pretty, but not beautiful. Her carefully pressed safari suit and styled brown hair marked her as a newcomer in the land of the pharaohs. Such efforts required a great deal of energy in the awesome desert climate. Anyone who had spent time here quickly learned to save their strength for sweating. Nevertheless, there was a quality of intelligence and determination in her face that Barrabas instantly respected.

"A young woman in distress. Nile, I want you to meet Anna Bockner, a medical researcher from Boston. Anna, Nile Barrabas, an old and honest friend. One of the few I have, actually."

Ratchett pulled a chair out for the woman and motioned for her to sit as the waiter brought the third glass.

"Anna arrived in Cairo this afternoon, and by late this evening had already found her way to me," Ratchett continued. "An extraordinary accomplishment in itself, Nile, as I'm sure you understand."

The woman smiled gently. "It was just a matter of persistence," she explained. "I'm indebted to one of the volunteers in our organization, Dr. Lee Hatton.

Dr. Hatton told me the person to see in Cairo was Al Ratchett, and if he couldn't help me, no one could.''

''Lee and I collaborated together once, years ago when she worked in Washington.'' Ratchett sighed. ''But all that's supposed to be a secret. A beautiful woman. I knew she'd left the agency, but I'd hadn't a clue what she's been up to until now.''

''She's gone ahead to Zaire,'' Bockner told the former British agent. ''To purchase supplies for the field trip and set up a protocol for collecting blood samples.''

Barrabas followed the conversation without comment, concealing his initial surprise. He knew Lee well. She worked for him. As the sole female member of the soldiers of Barrabas, she was a helluva fighter, and invaluable as the team's medic. Dr. Hatton often donated her time between jobs to development causes in Third World countries.

''Well, Anna is an expert in immunology and communicable diseases,'' Ratchett broke in, speaking directly to Barrabas. ''She's come here as part of an international team of experts to research an epidemic in equatorial Africa. Anna, why don't you tell Nile about the problems you're having.''

The woman squirmed slightly, somewhat uncomfortable with the idea. ''Well, I—''

Ratchett nodded at her. ''No promises, but he may be of some help.''

Bockner looked at Barrabas and began hesitantly. ''We're medical scientists from seven countries who've devoted ourselves to the greatest challenge facing medicine in the twentieth century. AIDS. Acquired immune deficiency syndrome.''

Barrabas was taken aback, baffled by Ratchett's implying a connection between this woman and his encounter in the neighborhood of the Zabalin earlier that evening.

"That's mostly in New York isn't it? A social disease spread by homosexuals?''

"No, Mr. Barrabas," Bockner interrupted sharply. "It's spread by a virus. In Africa, where it originated, everyone gets it, male and female, and its starting to spread like that in the United States as well. It was probably originally brought over by contaminated blood supplies. American hospitals buy a third of their blood from Third World countries.''

"So, what are you getting at? You're in Africa to prove this?''

"The origin is irrelevant, now that it's here. What we have to know is how it's transmitted. A group of researchers, based mainly in Boston, think the virus that has been discovered is only half the story. We think there's a connection to a type of very dangerous African swine fever virus called ASFV. It's spread by ticks. In the last ten years, wherever epidemics of ASFV in pigs have broken out, so has AIDS in humans. It's possible that pigs are reservoirs of the AIDS virus, which is then transmitted to humans by ticks that spread ASFV.

"We expected opposition from the medical establishment, of course. They're still blocking funding for a lot of the experiments and facilities we need for research. But when we tried to come to equatorial Africa to do research, we really ran into problems.''

Barrabas and Ratchett exchanged glances. The Brit had always had good instincts for connections. The young woman's story was beginning to sound interesting.

''First, we had trouble getting permission to come to Africa, and when we traced the problem somewhere deep inside the bowels of the State Department, the opposition suddenly evaporated. As if it were frightened off. So we sent a research team of six doctors here—a Canadian, two Frenchmen and three Americans, along with supplies for intensive blood testing of the African populations—human and pig. They came to Cairo.''

''And disappeared,'' Ratchett said in a low voice, feigning amazement. ''Vanished into thin air.''

Barrabas looked at Anna Bockner. She concealed her emotions well.

''We were told their airplane went down somewhere in the jungle. Parts of equatorial Africa still haven't been mapped, and the vegetation can camouflage small airplanes completely. But their supplies were supposed to follow them. They had been loaded into the cargo hold of another plane. That plane apparently never left the tarmac. And the material disappeared.''

Barrabas shrugged. ''Black marketeers. They saw an opportunity staring them in the face and went for it.''

''Possible,'' Ratchett said. ''But I checked with a few acquaintances who specialize in that area. There was some pretty sophisticated research equipment aboard. No one has seen anything like it on the black market. And that's unusual.''

Barrabas turned to Bockner. ''So what's next? You're here to find out what happened?''

The researcher sighed. ''Not officially. I'm here to accompany another shipment of research equipment on its way to Kinshasa in Zaire. The lives of my colleagues have been written off. But I can't leave it at that. I'm just anxious…anxious to know more about what might have…who might have…''

''I get it.'' Barrabas nodded. She was concealing it well, but she was obviously concerned for her own safety, not just the fate of her fellow scientists. ''When does the shipment go out?''

''Tomorrow,'' Ratchett answered. ''From the Heliopolis Aerodrome.''

''You're supposed to accompany it?'' he asked Bockner.

She nodded.

''Alone?''

''The other researcher couldn't make it at the last minute. And supposedly there's no danger.''

''What do you say, old chap?'' Ratchett looked closely at Barrabas.

The mercenary nodded slowly. ''Africa's an old stomping ground for me, Al.'' He faced Bockner. ''I'll go with you.''

''But…well, that's awfully kind of you, but I really can't afford…''

''Free!'' Ratchett proclaimed triumphantly. ''Protection! I love to wrap up a case. Your problems are solved. I would trust this man with my life, even though it's not worth half as much as yours, I dare say."

Barrabas leaned far across the table and squeezed Anna Bockner's shoulder reassuringly as he spoke. "I'm working on something, too. It might be related to what you're dealing with. If you can trust me, I'll help you out."

For a moment the woman considered his offer. Slowly she nodded. "Okay. Tomorrow morning at ten. At the aerodrome." She broke into a bright smile, tinged with relief, and waved to the nearby waiter for another round.

THEIR WAITER RETURNED to the bar and set his tray down in the service area. He called to the bartender who was busy shaking a drink.

"I must make a phone call! Two minutes!"

The bartender nodded wordlessly and strained the cocktail into glasses. The waiter disappeared through swinging doors into the employees' area and dropped coins into a pay phone. He waited two rings, then someone answered.

"They will be there," he said.

"Good." The phone at the other end clicked.

The waiter hung up and returned to the Sahara Club lounge.

**3**

By day, the sun's rays battled the layers of fine desert dust sifting across the city, and Cairo baked in a brownish haze.

The Heliopolis Aerodrome was a small commercial airfield near the Almaza and the international airports in the northeastern sector. It was the major North African depot for bushtraders, missionaries, humanitarians, carpetbaggers, explorers, scientists, poachers, smugglers, terrorists, freedom fighters and, of course, mercenaries—the flotsam that flew the airways across desert and jungle, traversing body and flesh of the Dark Continent.

Heat waves shimmered from the runways, distorting the languid movement of freight handlers and mechanics who wandered in and out of the cool shadows inside the great domed hangars.

She was waiting for him when he arrived at ten. A battered twin-prop Sparrow 37 was being wheeled outside. Mechanics in dirty blue overalls seemed to be fighting over the engine, waving handfuls of wrenches at the machinery and one another.

Bockner stood with her legs apart in a calf-length safari skirt, her hands on her hips. Sweat poured down her brow from under her safari hat, mixing with the fine air-blown dust and leaving trails down her skin. She was visibly upset. Her eyes thundered, and her bottom lip was stretched into a thin line. She looked like the school teacher about to ferret out the student with the whoopee cushion.

"It's already started!" she confided darkly. "The supplies were supposed to have been loaded. They aren't even here. Someone went to an office somewhere to try to find them. I know nothing more."

"Well, if someone's skimming them off before we even get out of here, I'm out of my league. I think you want to hire a private detective," Barrabas told her, dropping his kit bag and surveying the hangar. Open at both ends, it was a great corrugated tin Quonset, forty feet high at the center. The semicircular shape made it a perfect funnel for the winds blowing off the desert.

Wooden crates lay stacked in rows helter-skelter along the length of the hangar. Long worktables covered with tools and spare parts ran along the sides. An airplane had been taken apart at one end, bits of its metal innards carefully arranged in widening circles from the engine compartment. Everything was covered with a fine layer of silken dust. It was a miracle that anything worked in these desert countries.

"It could be a bureaucratic mix-up too. From what I hear, the Egyptian civil service is not a model of efficiency," he added, raising his voice to a yell as a small blue-and-white airplane tore overhead toward the landing strip. Another plane, white with a red flame streaking down the side, was taxiing past the hangár to a takeoff position. An overweight Egyptian man in a sweaty suit huffed and puffed through the heat and waved an armful of official-looking papers at them.

"I am truly sorry, but it's too late," he called to the medical researcher. "The instructions were changed. It's right here, here in these papers. There's nothing I can do, nothing."

Bockner spun around angrily. "What do you mean changed? By whom? When? What for?"

He pointed outside the hangar, where the plane with the red flame was gathering speed up the runway. "Last night orders came through for the consignment to be transferred to that plane. It was done!"

Bockner ripped the papers from the civil servant's hand and started to run, as if she were about to single-handedly stop the twin-prop aircraft from hurtling down the tarmac. The blue-and-white plane that had just landed taxied toward the hangar. Someone was waving from the cockpit. The mechanics gathered at the trough of the Sparrow 37 suddenly reached inside the engine compartment.

Barrabas dived forward, tackling Bockner at the waist. Guns sparked in the mechanics' hands, and the air was alive with bullets. One of them impacted, wrenching the woman from his arms. Sharp steel heat pierced his right leg, searing upward through his body. He collapsed, rolling crazily across the hangar floor as bullets pounded into the cement on all sides, spraying dust and sharp grit over him. As he fell behind a row of wooden crates, he freed the Browning from his shoulder holster.

His leg was numb, and a trail of blood streamed from a wound just above his ankle. But he was better off than Anna Bockner. He could see her through an opening between the crates, spread-eagled in a growing pool of blood. The mechanics, six of them, stood uncertainly outside the hangar.

The air vibrated with thunder from the engines of the blue-and-white airplane thirty feet away. It circled to face the hangar. One of the mechanics shouted an order, inaudible over the noise of the airplane. The killers quickly took cover on each side of the hangar entrance. The airplane door opened.

For a second, when Gunter Dykstra stuck his head from the plane and jumped to the tarmac, Barrabas's pain screamed back into him in slow motion as he watched a man who'd been a brother to him walk smiling into the arms of death.

Somehow Barrabas pulled himself up, digging his hands like talons into the wooden ribbing of the crates. When he put any weight on the wounded leg, the agony sucked his breath out.

He pushed himself from cover and hobbled several steps into the light outside the hangar entrance. Gunter saw him, and waved, his smile of greeting melting into a rictus of shock as he saw the Browning. Barrabas held it straight ahead of him, supporting it stiffly with his left arm. A gunman flashed from the seat of a nearby cargo lift, his gun pointed at Gunter's back.

Barrabas pivoted slightly on his good leg and fired. Two shots.

The man twisted into the air like a rag doll, jerked twice and dropped. Gunfire sounded on both sides.

Gunter turned to Barrabas, and their eyes met, milliseconds before the Dutchman's face exploded into a red death mask. He stumbled backward, his hands thrown into the air, and fell against the wheels of the airplane.

Barrabas spun to the left, the barrel of his gun birddogging the killer. Without warning, a steel club slammed against the back of his skull. All sensation drained from his body. He felt himself soar over the precipice of a great void and into the darkness of nonexistence.

MUSTAFA NALI WATCHED from the control tower while some of his men quickly and quietly cleaned the mess up at number five hangar. The Dutchman and the Egyptian mechanic whom the American mercenary had killed would be left for the local police to find; the files on Gunter Dykstra's background as a smuggler would be passed along. The dead attacker was well beyond questioning. As far as the local police were concerned, his motive would remain as mysterious as his identity.

A request for clearance came in from the pilot of the Sparrow. The Chief Air Traffic Controller, Mustafa Nali, had waived the flight-plan requirement. The surplus bodies were being airlifted out in the battered old plane that taxied up the runway, gathered speed and lifted from the ground. Soon it was a flyspeck, disappearing into the dusty yellow horizon over the Western Desert.

Nali left the tower in the charge of one of his subordinates and returned to his office in the aerodrome's administration building. Tersa was waiting for him, still dressed in his greasy blue mechanic's overalls. After the head controller had closed the door, he silently handed Nali a videocassette.

"Too bad about Mu'ad," he said. "I gave the order. But he was expendable. And the video is perfect." He unzipped the front of the overalls.

Nali walked around his desk and sat. For a moment he looked at the arrangement of the blotter, the clock, the telephone, the pictures of his healthy wife and smiling children. He inched one of the photos to the left.

He reached for the cassette.

"Good."

He swiveled around to face a television monitor and VCR on the credenza behind him. Tersa stepped out of his overalls uncovering a white shirt and European jeans. Heavy gold chains dangled from his neck and wrists. Lines flickered across the television screen as Nali inserted the cassette. The hangar appeared, with the old Sparrow outside and the gunmen running for cover. Gunter stepped from the airplane, and Barrabas stumbled outside. He fired, and Gunter's face disappeared in a bloody cloud. Suddenly Barrabas dropped like a stone and was still.

Nali flicked it off. "Excellent. We can cut right there."

"I'm a good cameraman. Worth the maximum you're paying me, isn't it? Look, you don't even see the guy sneak up behind him and lam him over the head with the crowbar."

"It's hard to believe it went so smoothly," Nali said. "So much depended on the timing. And apparently our timing was perfect."

He unlocked the right-hand drawer of his desk with a tiny key and withdrew a wad of American currency which he tossed across the desk toward Tersa.

"Five thousand dollars."

Tersa beamed as he picked it up and bounced it in his hand. He turned from the door to ask a last question. "Tell me, will I ever be told why your... benefactor... went to such elaborate extremes to produce this evidence?"

"No." Nali volunteered nothing further. He waited until Tersa was gone before putting the cassette in his briefcase. He had to deliver it to a highly placed official in the central government quarter by noon.

No explanation had been offered to Nali for evidence of a fabricated murder. But there was an old Egyptian proverb that covered most situations: when a man pays well enough, as this man did, he must have a very good reason.

BARRABAS RETURNED TO CONSCIOUSNESS, aware of a persistent vibration droning through him. Pain, steady and heavy, sat on his skull. His body felt sore, his stomach was nauseated, and a searing heat burned above his right ankle. He lay sideways, and his cheek rested against the hard, reconciling coolness of metal. The drone was from an engine. The airport. He was in an airplane. Barrabas opened his eyes.

Inches away, the blank eyes of the Boston researcher gazed nowhere. A neat bullet hole was visi-

ble in her temple, just above the swathe of drying
blood that caked her face and clothes. Her mouth was
open, but she had nothing to say, nor would she ever
again.

The American blinked, breathing slowly and deeply
to clear his head. The throbbing pain spilled into his
logical thoughts like water sloshing over the rim into
a bucket. He remained frozen in position, gradually
becoming aware that his hands had been bound but
not his legs.

He moved his wrists to test the bonds. They had
been tied with rough half-inch twine. He tightened and
relaxed the muscles of his arms, opening and closing
each hand several times. When the blood began to
flow, he tried to turn his wrists. They barely moved
inside the bonds, and the rope tightened, chafing
deeply against his skin. The knife strapped to the inside of his left calf would be useful. If he could get to
it. If it was still there.

Now he began to search with his eyes. He knew he
was in the fuselage of a small twin-prop airplane, a
cargo plane: the only light came from the blue sky beyond the cockpit windows. Just over the rise of Anna
Bockner's corpse he could make out the heads of the
pilot and co-pilot, in the cockpit. One leaned toward
the other to talk. Their words were inaudible under the
loud drone of the engines, but the laughter that followed was not.

They leaned back in their seats again, their backs
turned to their unwilling passenger.

Barrabas bent his left leg up behind him. Slowly he
arched back, straining down with his bound hands

until he was able to grab his pant leg. Moving his leg again, he pulled it down and groped along the straps of the nylon sheath. The knife was still there.

He twisted his fingers around the handle and straightened slowly. The knife slid smoothly from the sheath. He flipped it with infinite care between his fingers, like a baton twirler performing in slow motion, until the blade pointed up his body. He let go of it, felt the blade fall against the rope and his skin and quickly clenched the handle with the fingers of his right hand.

The awkward grip gave him about a half inch of cutting leeway, and the tip of the blade pressed against the thin skin on the upper side of his arm. He pulled his wrists as far apart as possible to tighten the rope, and he started cutting.

The thick, coarse twine gave easily, the bonds circling his wrists loosening quickly as the strands split and curled away from the knife. The blade broke his skin and dug painfully into his arm. The warm, sticky blood trickled over his fingers. They slipped on the handle, and the knife almost popped from his grasp. He lightened his grip, working on at the rope with a gentle sawing motion and straining to pull the rope tight.

Suddenly his wrists slipped six inches apart, and the knife dropped, falling with a dull metallic thud on the floor of the airplane. He closed his eyes as he caught movement in the cockpit, indicating the turn of a head.

Several strands of the thick twine still held, but with greater leeway he was able to reach the knife and grip it tightly in one hand. Before lifting it, he waited a moment, peering through the crack of his eyelids. The two pilots were in conversation, ignoring him again.

He lifted the knife and slashed. He was free.

The voices of the pilots rose suddenly above the noise of the engines. The copilot rose from his seat and turned back into the fuselage. He was short and swarthy, with dark hair and skin and a long, bushy mustache. The pilot shouted an instruction in Arabic. Holding on to a strap suspended from the ceiling, the copilot fiddled with the lock on the cargo door and pushed it open. Instantly, there was a loud whoosh as air was sucked out of the fuselage. The pilot's head twisted around and he shouted again over the deafening noise. The plane tipped sideways, the door gaping at the bottom of the incline. Barrabas slid down the smooth metal floor until his boots touched the wall.

The copilot moved slowly past the cargo door, hand over hand along the ceiling straps. He reached out his leg, pushing his army boot against Bockner's body, and shoved her toward the door. The corpse slid quickly down the metal floor and disappeared into space.

Carefully the copilot reached out to grab the next ceiling strap and moved farther down the fuselage until he stood over Barrabas. He planted his boot carefully between Barrabas's shoulder blades.

Barrabas whipped his arms up, driving the knife into the man's crotch and gripping his leg tightly with both hands. The Arab howled with shock and let go of the ceiling strap. With his foot against the wall for leverage, Barrabas threw the man toward the open cargo door. It was easy. The howl became a shriek of total terror as he tipped and plunged headlong into sky-blue emptiness. His last scream faded quickly. The twin engines whined as the small aircraft swung forty-five degrees. The pilot, white with panic, scrambled for his gun. He swung it over the back of his seat and fired.In the depressurized fuselage, the bullet's report was a soft muffled pop. Barrabas grabbed the handle of the cargo door, and kicked himself forward, vaguely aware of the bullet's trajectory past his forehead. He reached the cockpit, one arm circling the surprised pilot's neck in a stranglehold and the other grappling for the gun.

The pilot pulled back, trying to gain space to aim as Barrabas's fingers circled his wrist like steel pincers. With his hands off the controls, the airplane pitched forward and began to nose-dive, the engines screaming mightily as the two men became locked in silent combat.

The pilot pulled against Barrabas's grip, twisting the gun upside down, his knuckle whitening on the trigger as he aimed past his shoulder. The merc stared into the dark lidless eye of the barrel. He jerked the pilot's arm hard.

The gun roared, and the pilot shook as the bullet passed point-blank into his right temple. The top of his skull lifted like the lid of a pot. Blood, bone and brain boiled over, splattering the windshield and the instrument panel.

The airplane tipped almost ninety degrees as it screamed downward. For a moment, letting go of the pilot's mangled head, Barrabas was almost weight-less. Slowly he slid upward into the fuselage, his legs drifting toward the open cargo door. The plane began to twist and spiral as it dived, the blue horizon bob-bing in and out of the windshield view until it was re-placed by fast-approaching earth, a vast expanse of glaring white sand.

Parachutes were strapped to the ceiling over the cockpit seats. Fighting the gravitational force, Barra-bas grabbed the gory headrest of the pilot's seat and ripped a parachute down, pushing his forearm through the straps, and pulling it to his chest. He let go. Phys-ics did the rest.

He fell briefly against the thin aluminum wall until he was sucked through the opening. As he fell, he pulled the release cord.

The white fabric billowed out, catching the air like a cupped hand, the initial force jerking his arm away from his chest. His high-speed free fall halted, and he hung on for dear life as the descent began.

The ground below was so hot and white that it shimmered and glared. Heat rising in waves off the sand turned the desert into a crystalline ocean. It came up fast.

The American mercenary had made hundreds of jumps in his life, by day and by night. This time he had no markers, nothing to use to judge the point of im-pact in the alien landscape. Dangling from straps that should have been buckled around his waist and over his shoulders, it was impossible for him to maintain his body in the proper angle to utilize the parachute's braking power, or to make a proper landing.

When he hit, he hit hard, and flat on his back. He lay there, not breathing, numb from the impact, as the swathes of white parachute cloth gently floated down beside him. He filled his lungs and breathed. The sky was almost white, filled with blinding, searing sunlight. He closed his eyes against it, and it burned through the thin skin of his eyelids. He was lying on hard, baked sand. He made an effort to sit, but his stomach muscles refused to respond.

He felt no pain. The kind of chill that signaled serious trouble rippled through his chest. Nothing responded. He was totally numb, paralyzed. He couldn't move. He couldn't do anything but lie as he had fallen in the vast empty desert, where he would bake to death, shriveling up like a starfish beached at noon.

**4**

Transfixed by the two strangers, the shy African boy waited wide-eyed for an answer to his question.

"He asked, how does that white skin keep the rain out?" Dr. Lee Hatton laughed, translating from Swahili for the benefit of a mystified Alex Nanos.

Several dozen Bantu children had gathered in a circle at a safe distance from the two white Americans. Some were naked, some half dressed in ragged T-shirts, but like children everywhere in the world, they were both cautious of and curious about newcomers—especially these ones. Few people with white skins came to the town of Isipo in the eastern jungles of Zaire.

"*Mzungu!*" the little boy declared, pointing and then backing away, fearful that he might have unleashed some kind of danger.

"What did he say?" Nanos demanded, equally wary.

Lee laughed again. "*Mzungu.* It means novelty, something that's new and unusual. It's the Swahili word for white person."

Alex looked at her, dread crossed with amazement. It wasn't his first time in a strange place; he'd seen plenty stranger as one of the Soldiers of Barrabas. But this was a mission of mercy, not a routine covert-action assignment. And, for the first time, his contact with the natives was a little more intimate than the blood frenzy of a battlefield. Before they had left the United States two days earlier, Lee had told him it would do him good. He remained to be convinced.

In many ways the two mercenaries were as different as night and day. Dr. Hatton, a slender dark-haired woman of exceptional beauty, was the daughter of a famous deceased American general. She had earned her medical degree in the army women's corp, become an expert in the martial arts and gone on to a successful career working for a number of Washington's intelligence agencies. She had given it up to care for her invalid father at his Majorca villa until his death. That was where Nile Barrabas had found her when he was putting together the original covert-action team that came to be known as the Soldiers of Barrabas.

Alex Nanos was a party boy. Hailing from a Greek neighborhood in Chicago's tough east end, he had joined the Coast Guard after being expelled permanently from school. He had become one of their finest navigators before his unceremonious ousting. Too many rules had been broken, and too often in the company of a member of the opposite sex.

Broke and unemployed, the Greek had turned to what he knew best and had become a legend on the gigolo circuit from Boca Raton to Miami Beach. His recruitment into the SOBs hadn't exactly turned his life around, but the periodic assignments, the comradeship of the other mercs and the flirtation with death had given him a focus other than his usual one. Between wars Alex Nanos always returned to his forte—broads, booze and brawling.

It was quite the opposite for Lee Hatton. All the mercs had become wealthy enough to do pretty much what they wanted. Lee filled her time off with volunteer work.

"There's a time to live and a time to die," she'd explained to Nanos after their last antiterrorist mission with the SOBs. "I figure I put my time in with the killers, I should help out the victims, too."

This time she'd promised to assist a Boston-based international team of medical scientists who had encountered mysterious, almost insurmountable obstacles in their research on the greatest threat to public health in the twentieth century—AIDS. Dr. Hatton had challenged Alex Nanos to take a break from his usual activities and accompany her to Zaire in search of the origins of the terrible disease.

Alex Nanos was the first to admit it was out of character for him. But like the other SOBs, he'd been profoundly affected when Geoff Bishop, the Canadian who had served as a pilot for the team, had been killed on the last mission. Bishop's death was complicated by two things. He'd been Hatton's lover and Nanos's rival. And he'd died after a ten-hour ordeal in which he'd managed to save Alex's life.

Somehow, Bishop's death had created a bond between Hatton and Nanos that neither had expected. It had taken Alex more than a month to recover from burns and a serious bullet wound in his left shoulder.

Two days after he had passed Dr. Hatton's stringent physical, a twin-engine Cessna had flown them out of Kinshasa and deposited them eight hundred miles farther east, in the steaming equatorial jungles, in the uncharted heart of the Dark Continent.

Somewhere in the crowd of children, a bully shoved a tiny young girl forward. The child shrieked in panic and ran back to the protection of the others, where she hid fearfully behind a bigger girl. Lee squatted in front of the circle of children and held out her arm. Hastily they jumped back a foot like startled animals.

*"Jambo!"* she called to them, using a Swahili greeting.

The boy who had been brave enough to point and ask a question slowly put out his hand. He touched her quickly, barely brushing his fingers on hers before jumping back. *"Jambo,"* he said in a quiet voice.

Lee smiled at them, nudging Alex to do the same. The little audience burst into a chorus of childish giggles. The ice had been broken. Nanos relaxed and warmed to the moment.

"They're just like regular kids. I mean, American kids. I guess. I haven't talked to a kid in years."

"It gives you hope," Lee said, nodding. "Seeing how human beings are the same all over—at least as children. Makes you wonder why the grown-ups end up fighting."

A tall black man in casual slacks and a cotton shirt wandered in their direction. His dark coloring and high, rounded forehead marked him as a Bantu. Dr. Obispo—Dr. Sam as the villagers called him—had been trained at one of the finest medical schools in the

United States. Officially he was the Zairian government's chief medical officer in the region. In practical terms it was a grueling, low-paying job that required extensive travel through the bushlands in the eastern part of the country.

He smiled and shouted something in the native dialect, and the children scattered in all directions, giggling as if it were a game.

"We are ready for you now," he told the two Americans. "I will personally show you what you have come to see."

He led them through dusty streets, which ran between the rectangular mud houses with thatched roofs that made up the town of Isipo. The hospital was built of concrete blocks on floors of poured cement. It was neat and clean. With good reason Dr. Sam had a reputation for being one of Africa's finest public health authorities.

He led them to a bed at the far end of a long ward. A teenage girl used a stick with rags tied to the end to shoo flies from an emaciated woman who lay on the narrow bed, too weak to move.

"My God," Dr. Hatton murmured, glancing at the chart over the bed. The woman's age was listed as twenty-six. She looked sixty, her hair flecked with gray and her skin marred by myriad fungal infections. She had shrunk to barely fifty pounds, little more than a bag of bones. A sickly stench lay thick in the air. Silently Dr. Sam lifted the sheet covering the woman's leg. It was gangrenous almost to the hip.

"We amputate tomorrow," he explained. "She's been ill for more than two years."

Nanos turned away, almost sick to his stomach. "That's AIDS?" he asked, choking on the words.

The tall Zairian doctor shrugged. "We don't know what we're dealing with really. We don't have the equipment to do the right testing. But, yes, probably. The immune system is wiped out, leaving the body open to all kinds of infections that do not bother healthy people."

"Your immune system is like a gun," Lee explained to Alex. "When a foreign agent—a germ or a virus—comes along, it shoots to kill. But the AIDS virus gets inside the system. Then it's like when you aim your gun to fire on an attacker, your gun blows up in your hand instead."

"An excellent analogy," Dr. Sam commented, leading them from the ward. "Here in Zaire it's called the Horror, and it's spreading quickly. And because we're so helpless to stop it, many of the native people are turning to traditional folk remedies administered by witch doctors, or the men who run the Croix Rouge outposts in the outlying villages."

"I didn't know the Red Cross was extensively involved here," Hatton said.

Dr. Sam shook his head. "They're not, at least, not the same organization. These are men who are hastily trained as paramedics by the government and licensed to treat people. They set up little dispensaries in villages and give people what they want—usually something they can feel, like adrenaline or vitamins, and always with a syringe. People here figure if it doesn't give them a kick, it doesn't work. Unfortunately, most of the Croix Rouge use a single, unsterilized needle for dozens of patients. That's one of the major ways this disease is being spread here in Africa. I have to make a tour of some small villages farther east. How do you two feel about an overnight trip into the jungle?''

The two mercs exchanged glances. Nanos nodded. "Why not?"

"Definitely," Lee said. "My colleague is leaving Cairo today, so she won't get here until tomorrow evening sometime."

"We'll be back well before then," Dr. Sam said. "Actually, I'm glad to have you along. I've been hearing strange rumors from the bush. Some of the witch doctors have been urging the people to destroy the Croix Rouges, and anything else remotely affiliated with Western medicine. Professional jealousy, I'd say, fanned by panic because of this disease. And there are the usual stories of evil spirits in the jungle visiting villages to make people sick. I hope there's no confrontation when I show up. Having two *mzungu* along will undoubtedly be of help."

"How do we travel?" Nanos asked. He had yet to see a vehicle since the Cessna had landed an hour before. The heat was so severe their faces were beaded with sweat, and their clothing was damp and heavy. He didn't relish the idea of walking.

Dr. Sam motioned them to follow him outside toward the rear of the hospital building. A battered Land Rover was parked on the dusty sand road. Beside it, a half-dozen two-gallon cans marked Petrol were neatly stacked.

"By road—of sorts," the Zairian doctor told them, glancing at his watch. "We leave in fifteen minutes."

When the all-terrain vehicle was loaded with gasoline, drinking water, medicines, cots and mosquito netting and a portable shortwave radio, Hatton and Nanos climbed aboard, with Dr. Sam behind the wheel.

"No food?" Alex questioned, casting a baleful eye over the practical supplies in back. He and Dr. Hatton had decided to leave most of their gear in Isipo. Nanos had hastily packed a single duffel bag with rain gear, a change of clothing, and against Lee's wishes, the two 9 mm Heckler and Koch submachine guns they'd brought from America and smuggled through Zairian customs. Like the Boy Scouts, he rationalized. Always be prepared.

"You will have an opportunity to experience Zairian hospitality," Dr. Sam told him. "At each village we will be fed the best of what they have to offer. Sometimes this will be only *fou-fu*, but to refuse it would be to insult them terribly."

*"Fou-fu?"* Nanos wrinkled his nose and looked at Lee.

"Manioc," she said. "The root of a tree dried, then moistened again into a thick gooey paste."

"And if we are lucky, a stew made from monkey meat!" Dr. Sam exclaimed, laughing at Alex's discomfort.

"They eat monkeys!"

The Zairian health officer nodded, his voice darkening. "There is nothing else. You will see."

The rutted sandy road led through miles of dry bushland, cut by impenetrable stands of elephant grass. Rolling green foothills rose to the Mitumba Mountains farther east, marking Zaire's border with the small African republic of Burundi, forty odd miles away. For a long time the three travelers rode without speaking as the Land Rover bounced over the rough trail. Eventually the jungle closed in on both sides with a mysterious silence.

"There are no animals," Alex said, awed and disconcerted. "Not even birds!"

Dr. Sam nodded. "Killed off in the colonial wars. Eaten. The people are hungry, and the population doubles with each generation. The jungles have become silent. Sometimes there are monkeys. That is all."

By late afternoon they arrived at Shibandu, their first village, a collection of thatched mud houses. An ancient dumpster roared past them with dozens of dead bloodied monkeys tied by their tails and swinging from the sides of the vehicle like clumps of garlic. The Land Rover stopped outside the tiny health center as the natives on the truck threw down the tailgate. The back of the truck was piled high with dead monkeys. Laughing and joking, the natives on board began shoveling the dead animals onto the ground.

Villagers streamed from their houses and filtered out of the elephant grass. Several of them—the *infirmiers* who ran the health center, and the village leaders—hurriedly approached the surprise delegation from Isipo. But most rushed toward the battered truck that had returned from the monkey hunt, casting the two *mzungu* odd, apprehensive looks. Dr. Sam was quickly swept into a frenzy of ritual greeting.

Nanos and Hatton drifted to the side, momentarily forgotten, as a mildly cooling breeze swept in from somewhere, drying the dusty sweat on their faces.

"What are you thinking?" Lee asked the Greek, watching his face.

Alex came back from his thoughts, but hesitated.

"About that woman with AIDS in the hospital in Isipo," he admitted. "The look in her eyes. I've been trying all afternoon to figure out where I've seen that look before, and I just realized it. Sometimes, you know, when we've been attacked, and you're looking into the whites of the enemy's eyes, and you're just about to blow his head off. That's when I've seen the look. It's like this instant desperation, and then it's gone—" Nanos snapped his fingers. "Like that. Because you blow his head off. It was that kind of look, except with that poor woman, it wasn't instant. It was like, trapped inside her, she was fighting but knowing that the only thing that's going to set her free is to surrender. You know, die. I dunno, Lee, I can't explain it very well."

Lee Hatton looked at the Greek almost in amazement. "Alex, in all the time I've known you, I've never heard you explain anything so articulately."

"Artikyouwhat?"

She smiled, shaking her head. "Never mind."

Dr. Sam pushed his way through the small crowd that had greeted him near the infirmary and strode over to the two Americans. For the first time Hatton noticed that another group of villagers had gathered off to one side. They were eyeing the Americans with thinly veiled hostility and murmuring among themselves. Dr. Sam was clearly disturbed.

"Something very strange is going on," he told them angrily. "The village is on the verge of civil war, with supporters of the man who runs the Croix Rouge against my people who run the government health center. The man who runs the Croix Rouge here started collecting blood samples after the first cases of the Horror struck this village. He ran off into the jungle as soon as he saw I was coming here."

"He's not supposed to?" Alex queried.

"Oh, they always run away when I come. It's the blood samples. It's unheard of. And that's not all. Come on. Let's have a look."

Not waiting for an answer, Dr. Sam grabbed a flashlight from the Land Rover and took off across the road, heading for a stick and mud-daubed hut at the far edge of the village. The door was covered by a dirty sheet with a huge freehand red cross roughly painted on it. The African thrust the sheet aside and went in, Hatton and Nanos right behind him.

"I don't know what's normal here and what's not," Alex commented in frustration, seeing trays of instruments, packages of drugs and several hypodermic needles sitting in a jar of water.

"That's not." Dr. Sam looked grim as he shone his flashlight on a shiny enamel refrigerator standing against one wall.

"There's no electricity within hundreds of miles!" Nanos exclaimed.

"It runs on kerosene," Dr. Sam said gruffly, grasping the handle and pulling it open. His flashlight shone on rows of small test tubes, each one filled with blood and topped by a rubber stopper.

"What in hell's going on?" Lee muttered, looking at her Zairian colleague, whose face twitched with controlled fury.

Dr. Sam shook his head. "I was told that one day, several weeks ago, this refrigerator appeared overnight. It was the wonder of the village because no airplanes or trucks from outside had been here in months. Magic, the villagers were told. Then they were told by the man in the Croix Rouge that if he took a bit of their blood into the jungle, helpful spirits will magically bless it to protect them from the Horror."

"You're right, Sam," Dr. Hatton said, making a connection to the troubles that the Boston-based medical scientists had in trying to launch their research project in Africa. "Something is not right."

"Sounds to me like the answers are out there in the jungle," Nanos said.

Dr. Sam nodded. "It's evening now, and too late to do anything. But I think we should find some of these so-called jungle spirits and ask them a question or two first thing in the morning."

5

The next day the mercs rose at the first glimmer of dawn. For the second time since dinner the night before, Nanos made a valiant effort to keep down some of the glutinous *fou-fu*. By the time they met Dr. Sam at the Land Rover in front of the infirmary, the village was slowly coming to life.

The Zairian health official introduced them to a smiling teenager named Seku.

"He was hunting monkeys several days ago when he became separated from the other men and had to spend the night in the jungle. While he was up in a tree by the road, he saw the man who runs the Croix Rouge walking away from the village. Several hours later, a van or a truck drove in that direction. But the road doesn't lead anywhere."

"In that case, where does the road go?" Nanos asked.

"First, the word 'road' is almost a misnomer." Dr. Sam reached into the Land Rover for a map, which he spread over the hood. "It's more of a sandy trail. It leads to an old open-pit copper mine, abandoned thirty years ago by the colonialists who ruled Zaire when it was known as the Belgian Congo. It's thirty-five miles or so from here in the mountains along the border with Burundi.'' The young African boy spoke something rapidly to Dr. Sam in his native dialect. The doctor smiled. ''He says we're lucky it's the dry season, because in the rainy season the road is impassable.''

''If we're lucky we might be able to do fifteen miles an hour then,'' Lee commented, climbing into the Land Rover. She had had enough experience with African roads to make the shrewd guess. Nanos heaved his duffel bag over his shoulder into the back of the vehicle. The automatic weapons inside it clunked heavily on the floor.

''Insurance policy,'' he replied to Dr. Sam's questioning stare, as he climbed behind the wheel.

The sun was just above the horizon when they left the village, already hot as it began its searing equatorial trek straight overhead. For ten miles the Land Rover heaved and lurched in and out of potholes and dried ruts as the road passed through sparse jungle. Seku showed them the tree he had climbed when he had seen the vehicle drive past, and several times they stopped to examine the remnants of tire tracks in the sandy soil. The chevron marks pointed in both directions, indicating that what had passed one way had also returned.

Two and a half hours later the vegetation thinned, opening into a wide plain of elephant grass, dotted occasionally with flat broad-leaved trees. Several miles ahead of them, the land began rolling upward to the Burundi border. The land rising on the horizon still bore traces of green from the rainy season but had begun to fade to a parched yellowish brown, almost matching the uniform color of the sandy soil. Like the jungle they had passed through the day before, the land was eerily silent, devoid of birds and animal life.

"Beyond those mountains," Dr. Sam told them pointing to the Mitumba Mountains in the east, "you will find one of the sources of the mighty river Nile."

"I thought the Nile was in Egypt," Nanos said, turning from the wheel. The all-terrain vehicle hit a deep pothole, throwing the travelers a foot off their seats.

"Well, yes," the Zairian said, laughing. "But its southernmost source is in Burundi, where it starts small, gathering strength and size as it flows north four thousand miles."

"As long as it took to discover it," Lee murmured. "For four thousand years people—even the entire Roman army—tried with no luck."

"That's right," said Dr. Sam. "Pharaohs, caesars and emperors with all their power and glory tried and failed, until 1937. An impoverished German explorer discovered it on his own."

"No kidding," Alex said. The Land Rover hit another bump, jolting the words from his mouth and the steering wheel from his hands. A loud whine of protest issued from the angry transmission.

Dr. Sam unfolded the map again, calculating in his head the distance they had traveled. Lee looked over his shoulder. They were about five miles from the spot that marked the location of the old copper mine.

"It's here, I believe," Dr. Sam said, "in a small valley between two hills."

"I think we should hide the Land Rover and trek overland," Lee suggested. "Then we can have a look from the top of the first hill."

"Good idea," Nanos agreed. He braked, scanning the terrain around them for some kind of cover. He pointed to a copse not far off the road. "How about leaving the Rover in there?"

They refreshed themselves with rations of water, and Lee produced a cache of energy-giving raisins that she had secreted in her knapsack. Seku piled brush against the sides of the Land Rover to hide it from the trail. Nanos opened his duffel bag and withdrew the two H&K submachine guns and a dozen mags of 9 mm ammunition.

"What have you brought?" Dr. Sam exclaimed, suddenly angry at the sight of the deadly weapons. Seku lingered beside Nanos's elbow, his teenage curiosity at once intimidated and intrigued by the sleek shiny metal.

"Insurance," Alex told the Zairian doctor, fitting a mag into each gun.

"But these are not necessary. It's my job to save lives, not to watch people kill each other!"

Lee Hatton moved between the two men, taking the gun that Nanos proffered. "Believe me, Sam, it's our job, too. But unless you have an ironclad explanation for what we saw in the Croix Rouge hut yesterday, I think we should be prepared for all contingencies."

Grudgingly Dr. Sam moved away. "I do not approve." He started off by himself in the direction they had chosen.

Nanos looked at Hatton. "I'll take point. Maybe you can talk him down."

Lee nodded. She took a pair of binoculars from the Land Rover and motioned Seku to fall into line while she caught up with Dr. Sam. They walked in silence. Nanos ran ahead, disappearing in and out of the thick thornbushes that covered the hillside.

Although the incline was gradual, the ascent was hot work. The equatorial sun was suspended. The two mercs were soon perspiring heavily and even Dr. Sam's face was beaded with sweat. Only Seku seemed unaware of the heat.

The thornbushes soon gave way to short, stiff grass and rocky outcroppings, and the mountains of the eastern border loomed higher as they approached the summit. The top of the hill was almost flat, the edge of the far side a precipice framing the valley below. Nanos was waiting for them as they made the last haul and stopped to catch their breath.

"There's a pit mine down there," he told them. "But it sure don't look abandoned to me." He threw Lee a sharp private look. "Have a look, but stay down."

Dr. Sam ordered Seku to sit while the three adults crawled to the brink of the hill. Hatton raised the binoculars to her eyes.

The valley was lined with steep cliffs of brown rock that rose at nearly ninety-degree angles on three sides. At the bottom, the rutted road led through a pass to the old copper mine, a rounded excavation resembling a ruined amphitheater, fifty feet deep and a quarter of a mile across. But the sight of the old mining camp left Hatton and Dr.Sam speechless.

A string of wooden barrack-type buildings that might once have housed African workers now had camouflaged roofs. On one side, on a plateau of rock jutting from the hillside an immense house had been built in the style of a French château from the native brown rock. Once, it had housed a manager, his family and other Europeans. Part of it was in ruins, but the main wing was obviously well cared for, and lived in.

More surprising was the array of vehicles parked in a flat area along the edge of the pit. There were several jeeps and pickup trucks, some electric dolly carts, and two Bell six-seater helicopters that looked brand-new. Most of the vehicles were covered with camouflage netting. The choppers were painted in splotches of tan and loden green. Someone had taken a lot of precautions to make sure the camp wasn't visible from the air. As she watched, Lee saw a number of men leave the big house and walk toward the workers' barracks. They held clipboards and talked among themselves. One gesticulated rapidly with his hands, as if he were trying to make a point. They had white skin.

There were Africans down there, too—dozens of them dressed in anonymous green uniforms. Some appeared to be servicing some of the vehicles. Others worked outside the barracks, moving rounded aluminum cases on a battery-powered dolly toward one of the helicopters. But most of them patrolled the open areas in and around the camp. They were heavily armed with Africa's weapon of choice—AK-47 assault rifles.

Hatton ran the field glasses along the buildings, making out ventilation chimneys, a gasoline storage depot and a building that appeared to house an electrical generator. There was an enormous refrigeration unit outside one of the buildings. A satellite dish beside the stone house was almost completely obscured by camouflage netting.

"Some operation," she said quietly to the others, handing the glasses to Dr. Sam.

"Check out the firepower?" Nanos asked.

Lee nodded.

Dr. Sam whistled in amazement, and lowered the field glasses. "I can assure you, this is no operation of the government of Zaire."

"What about neighboring countries, Burundi or Rwanda?" Nanos suggested. "We're near the border, and frontiers are pretty vague in Africa, aren't they?"

Dr. Sam shook his head. "I cannot imagine. We are looking at something that has cost millions of dollars, and those governments do not have that kind of money to spend. But what is it? A secret military operation?"

"Heiss," Lee Hatton said, abruptly. "Karl Heiss."

Nanos looked at her, his brows raised in silent query. It was a radical suggestion. What would Nile Barrabas's nemesis be doing here?

She shrugged. "A gut feeling. Call it woman's intuition, call it whatever you want, but that's what it feels like to me."

"Who is this man Heiss?" Dr. Sam asked quickly.

"The personification of evil. Sam, how does that radio in the Land Rover work?"

"I tune into the missionary network that exists across central Africa. For ten minutes after the hour every hour, a satellite listens for transmissions from the bush and relays them to a central facility in Nairobi. Messages are relayed to Europe and America from there."

The woman doctor looked at her watch. It was twenty minutes to one. She turned to Nanos. "Code yellow for Jessup. We've got half an hour to get down the hill."

THE DESCENT WAS RAPID, but by the time the mercs and the two Zairians reached the Land Rover, they were breathing heavily, enervated by the heat and soaked in sweat. Seku quickly began pulling the brush away from the vehicle. Dr. Sam handed Alex Nanos a coiled wire antenna.

"We can use that tree," he suggested, pointing to the one nearest the vehicle.

They carried the radio ten feet from the truck. Alex climbed to the first limb, and Lee threw the antenna to him. He draped it over the branch and began to wind it around the main trunk, handing it down to Hatton, who finished uncoiling it. Following Dr. Sam's instructions, Seku pounded a stake into the ground and attached a second wire to it as a ground.

Dr. Sam started the Land Rover and drove it up beside the radio. Leaving the engine idling, he opened the hood and attached cables to the battery terminals. He pulled them over the fender and plugged them into cables trailing from the back of the radio.

"Do you mind telling me just who you're contacting," he asked Hatton, bending over the radio to adjust the dials.

The American doctor squatted beside him, watching his hands carefully turn the dial to find the correct frequency. It was eight minutes after one. They had two minutes. She put her hand on his shoulder and spoke earnestly.

"We have a friend. His name isn't important. My guess might be totally off the wall, but that operation up there looks to me like the work of a renegade CIA agent named Karl Heiss. Our friend has dealt with him before. The only way we can contact him is through an office in New York. Once we get the word through, they'll know what to do. But if we try anything ourselves, well, I have the feeling we're already in very great danger."

A small red light above the dial flickered, then beamed steadily, and static erupted from the earphones. Dr. Sam turned down the dial and put them on.

Speaking slowly, and clearly, he spoke into the mouthpiece. "Mission Network, this is GMQ3ZN, I say again, Golf Mike Quebec Three Zulu November. Do you read?"

After a short pause, he repeated his code. He looked at Hatton, shaking his head. No response. Lee glanced at her watch. One minute. She automatically did something she'd been doing in tight situations since childhood: she crossed her fingers. Dr. Sam repeated his call letters once again. They waited.

Suddenly the light flickered, and a rush of static in Dr. Sam's ears made him wince. He nodded. They were through.

"Standby, network control." He removed the headset and handed it to Lee. "Say 'message for' and the name of the agency or person in New York. Then repeat the message. That's it."

Carefully Lee followed his instructions, repeating the name Walker Jessup and the contact telephone number that gave the mercs direct and immediate access to his office.

Walker "The Fixer" Jessup was an enormous Texan and former intelligence operative who, through his private consulting company and for a generous percentage, relayed mission-oriented messages to the SOBs from the American government. Nanos handed her the folded map with the coordinates of Shibandu written in the margin.

The rest of the message was succinct. Code yellow would initiate the process of locating Nile Barrabas and the other SOBs. They would be contacted and put on alert, ready to move out. Hatton had barely finished the message when the signal began to fade. The red light blinked, and a few seconds later the transmitter was silent.

She heaved a sigh of relief.

The end of the antenna with its plastic insulator landed at her feet, and Nanos hopped down from the tree.

"We've got to get out of here fast, and far enough back to civilization to find a telephone," she said. "I've got to fill New York in on the details before we decide what to do next."

With Seku's eager help, Nanos lugged the heavy radio to the Land Rover, and they lifted it into the back. From somewhere in the scrub brush, a bird warbled softly and was answered by its mate. For a moment they hardly noticed it.

Nanos's and Hatton's eyes met.

"No birds," Alex said, reaching for his H&K submachine gun as Hatton grabbed hers.

Dr. Sam and Seku looked at them, surprised. There was movement in the elephant grass, the whipping sound of cloven air and Seku was suddenly thrown off his feet. He fell back against the tree, a long spear protruding from his gut. The boy squirmed silently, his hands kneading the shaft that impaled him until he fell forward, dead.

Hatton felt a sharp steel point press into her back. It tore her shirt as she spun around, pressing into her flesh and forcing her back over the hood of the Land Rover.

"I wouldn't do that!" a deep voice boomed with deadly authority.

She twisted to see Nanos and Dr. Sam immobilized. The blades of long spears pressed into their throats, forcing them back over the sides of their vehicle. A second spear was pressing into Nanos's arm, forcing his gun high into the air.

The elephant grass parted, and a dozen African men surrounded them. They wore the dark green uniforms of the encampment on the other side of the hill. Their eyes were fierce, and their burnished black skin glistened with sweat. Half of them carried spears; the other half were armed with AK-47s.

Suddenly Dr. Sam twisted away from the spear at his throat, and turned for the elephant grass in a blind panic. A big man, taller and broader than the others, wearing leopard skin epaulets on his shoulders, stepped forward. His arm moved, and the silver blade of a long knife flashed, coming down on Dr. Sam in a single blow. The Zairian's head split in half like a ripe melon, and he dropped dead instantly. The leader pulled the bloody machete up, wiping it on the back of Dr. Sam's shirt. He smiled and flicked his hand.

Quickly the soldiers with the guns stepped past the ones with the spears to disarm the mercs.

"Usually," the tall African leader said, pronouncing each syllable with careful precision, "the boss no want the busybody visitor. But this time, with *mzungu*, we see. Maybe he like someone to play with." His white teeth gleamed. "Or maybe he give them to us!"

**6**

Erika Dykstra's heels clicked on the tile floor as she strode steadily down the long corridor of the Cairo hospital. The Egyptian detective waited for her by the nursing station. He was a stout, square-shouldered man, balding, but with a gracious smile.

"My deep regrets, Madame Dykstra. That this tragedy should occur in my country is a matter of great shame, not only for me, but for all—"

"Thank you, Mr. Kadry."

"Ahmed, please. May I inquire as to your brother's condition?"

Erika blinked away the tears that welled in her eyes. She had caught the first available flight out of Schipol Airport and had arrived in Cairo a day after the incident. Her beautiful face was pale, lined by strain.

The doctors had little to say. Gunter had lost most of his face in the gun blast. It could be reconstructed by plastic surgeons in expensive European clinics, if he came out of the coma, which they doubted. He lay in a bed in the al-Azhar University Hospital, swathed in bandages, immobile and as lifeless as a mummy.

"Unchanged," Erika told the government official.

He had appeared at the hospital unbidden while she was in her brother's room.

"I apologize for pressuring you at this delicate moment, Madame Dykstra, but we are conducting an investigation. May I ask you to accompany me to my office where it might be possible for you to answer a few questions."

"What could I possibly tell you?" she responded, her anger sparked by emotional exhaustion. "The police report states that he was caught in a cross-fire during a gunfight between illicit arms dealers or drug smugglers. I can assure you, Gunter did not come to Egypt for either of those reasons."

Ahmed Kadry smiled kindly. "Of course, *madame*. But some additional, possibly urgent evidence has been uncovered. It's possible your brother was deliberately set up."

Erika stared, suddenly repulsed by the man who seemed to thrive on her brother's misfortune like a cockroach scuttling after crumbs in a grubby kitchen.

"I haven't even checked into a hotel yet. I don't even have a reservation."

"I assure you, it will only take a few minutes. My office is downtown. And I will be glad to take you to a hotel afterward. Indeed, I'll have one of the secretaries make a reservation for you while we discuss the situation."

He extended his arm, a gentlemanly gesture motioning her ahead. A few minutes later they were jammed into the heavy Cairo traffic. The cool interior of Kadry's air-conditioned, chauffeur-driven car was a relief. The Egyptian appeared to be high-ranking. Erika didn't like it. The car made its way slowly through the tightly packed streets of the business district to the government quarter near the river. The driver pulled up outside a massive square building of coral-pink sandstone, one of the great administrative edifices erected by Nasser after the revolution of 1952. Erika followed Kadry down long corridors that led through the bureaucratic headquarters.

"I am a detective," the Egyptian explained, "but also the senior commander for the airport militia. Naturally, my jurisdiction overlaps with that of the local police, particularly inside the municipal boundaries of Cairo. Part of my job, however, is to oversee security arrangements. One of our recent innovations at the Heliopolis Aerodrome was the installation of a sophisticated video surveillance system in response to a dramatic increase in pilfering."

He showed her into a wood-paneled room, where he moved toward a large desk littered with papers. With a wave of his arm, he invited her to sit in a gilded chair, the Egyptian colonial version of a French antique. It was highly uncomfortable.

Kadry opened the top drawer of his desk and pressed some buttons. A television strategically placed on a low table sprang to life. The detective quickly closed the venetian blinds and pulled the thick drapes with the woven Islamic design tightly shut. He sat in the chair beside Erika, folded his hands in his lap and looked at her carefully.

"The local police were not aware of this, of course, since we have evidence to believe they are involved in the pilfering, and the surveillance system was designed to entrap them as well as others.''

"What are you getting at?" Erika asked sharply. Her suspicions had been raised, not merely by the mysterious airs put on by the detective, but by the timing of this interview. The other civil servants had left for the day. Not even secretaries in the outer office were present.

"I mean, Madame Dykstra, that your brother's . . . accident was captured on videotape, and I believe it clearly indicates the man who shot him. It is in the hope that you might identify this man that I have asked you to accompany me here."

Ahmed Kadry's eyes wandered toward the television screen. Erika followed. She saw her brother, smiling, emerge from the small airplane and wave at someone. Then her heart leaped into her throat, and the blood in her veins became ice. Barrabas's short-cropped white hair was unmistakable the moment he emerged from the hangar. She watched the gun he held fire and her brother fall wounded to the ground. The video ended abruptly. Kadry pressed a remote, and the set went blank.

"The videotape ran out," the detective told her. "We were lucky to have recorded what we did."

Erika sat perfectly still, silent, her mind racing through the horrible possibilities.

Kadry spoke again. "Do you know this man, the one with the white hair who fired the gun?"

She thought a moment, then turned sideways in the awkward chair to face the Egyptian steadily. "No," she said firmly, speaking almost between clenched teeth. "I've never seen him."

Kadry reached over to his desk and lifted a thin file folder. "A passport check of visitors entering the country in the days immediately prior to the event indicate an American of this description named—" he flipped open the file and read from a page in front of him "—Nile Barrabas. He left the country before we could talk to him. Passport control indicates he caught a flight to Kinshasa, the capital of Zaire, an hour after the shooting." The detective closed the file and looked at Erika.

"I've never heard Gunter mention that name," she told him evenly, standing to leave. "I'm sure he must be someone my brother never knew."

For a long time, Erika sat on the bed in her hotel room, her mind empty. The shocking events—first Gunter's terrible wound, and second, Ahmed Kadry's questioning—had initially filled her with anxiety and turmoil. Now these feelings had abated, leaving behind a chilling, dreadful calm.

She did not stir until the fast-falling shadows of dusk filled the room with darkness, and the streetlights of Cairo began to glow through the dusty yellow twilight. Her brother, she knew, was as good as dead.

She stood and walked to the luggage near the door. After tearing off the baggage ties on the top suitcase, she opened it, rifled through her hastily packed clothing and withdrew from its hiding place the small, silver handled revolver that she always carried when she traveled abroad. Although she knew it was loaded, she doubled-checked. Six bullets. One of them for her brother's murderer. And enough left over for anyone who got in the way.

She put the gun down on a nearby table and picked up the telephone.

"Hello, operator. Air Africa please. Yes? Hello. I'd like to book a seat on a flight to Kinshasa. As soon as possible. Yes, I'll hold. Thank you."

AHMED KADRY PULLED AT HIS TIE to loosen it as he reached for the ringing telephone. He recognized his benefactor's thin, obstreperous voice immediately.

"The bait has been set," Kadry said slowly. "It only remains to be seen if the prey takes it."

"She has," the voice whined through a burst of static on the line that stretched from equatorial Africa. "My sources at Air Africa have just informed me. You've performed very well, Ahmed. It's difficult to believe that everything worked out so perfectly."

"You left the matter in competent hands," the detective commented pointedly. "There was a small matter. The airplane disappeared yesterday. Apparently it went down in the Western Desert."

"It what?"

"It's of no consequence. The crash undoubtedly destroyed the bodies." Kadry could hear his benefactor breathing hard—with anger or excitement it was impossible to tell.

"It concerns me. Cats are not the only creatures with nine lives." The thin voice was barely audible through another burst of equatorial static. The Egyptian failed to understand the obscure reference to cats.

"You needn't worry," Ahmed Kadry said soothingly. "I have ensured there will be no search party. And no one survives the Western Desert for long."

Four thousand miles from Cairo Ahmed Kadry's benefactor returned the telephone receiver to its cradle. He sat back in the plush leather chair, with his hands folded neatly on the desk in front of him. A ceiling fan spun in the dark wood-paneled study. It was midafternoon, but the louvered shutters had been closed tightly against the equatorial heat, and only a thin glimmer of light trickled through. A small bronze lamp with a green glass shade glowed on the corner of the desk, casting its light away from him and leaving his features in shadow. The Belgians had built the great stone house with a fondness for memories of their distant European home. He might well be sitting in the study of a French château instead of in a great stone house built on the edge of an abandoned copper mine near the Zaire-Burundi border.

For a few moments he remained perfectly still, his mind mulling over the progress he had made. Despite the clockwork precision with which his plans were unfolding, two loose ends had appeared. One loose thread could unravel the entire fabric, he knew, and he could not eliminate completely the possibility that events might yet fall from his control.

He disliked loose ends. Were they a normal part of the elaborate scheme, which by its very nature must produce unforeseen consequences? Or were they the beginning of something else? Was someone trying to stop him?

He had never been more invulnerable; he had never had a greater network of support or more powerful backers. But this time he would not eliminate any possibilities, no matter how remote. He had failed before—invariably because of the efforts of the man who was his greatest enemy, the man whom Kadry assured him was dead in Egypt's Western Desert. That was the first loose end. He wanted to gaze at the corpse of Nile Barrabas. Ahmed Kadry would be instructed to find the body or else.... A smile glimmered on the face of the man at the desk. He would think of something persuasive. He could be quite creative in that respect.

The second loose end was far more disturbing. He thought of the old adage—the first time is chance, the second coincidence, the third enemy action. He adjusted the lampshade so that the light glared into the room, then pressed a button on his telephone.

A moment later the tall, strapping African with the leopard-skin epaulets entered the room. He stood at attention before the desk, blinking against the bright light that shone across his ebony skin.

"Banu reporting, sir." The black soldier saluted stiffly.

"At ease, Commander." His voice came from the cool obscurity of shadows behind the desk, precise and deliberate.

The African swallowed nervously. He put his hands behind his back and stood very straight.

"Do you have any idea who these prisoners are?"

"Yes, sir! It appear the two Zairians killed is Dr. Sam Obispo, regional public health officer for the government of the Republic of Zaire, and a boy from the village."

"Yes, I already know that. The man who operates the Croix Rouge informed us of it when he reached here this morning. I mean the two Americans."

"No, sir. My men want to execute immediately. I prevent it. It is so very unusual for *mzungu* to enter eastern jungles. I think you might have something to ask before they die."

There was a pause in the conversation, timed by the rhythmic whir of the overhead fan. The man behind the desk slid his chair smoothly back on oiled casters and rose. The glare from the lamp obscured Commander Banu's vision, but he saw the dark shape of a thick-shouldered man of medium height walk with extreme rigidity to the shuttered windows. In his tribe parents told their children of a nasty jungle spirit who ate babies, had no neck and could see by turning his head in all directions. Banu had not seen this man eat babies and, indeed, no longer believed in the primitive superstitions of the tribes, but the man had no neck, and had eyes to see for him all over the world.

Banu's boss carefully opened the louvers of one shutter a crack and peered through the glass, squinting for a moment against the brilliant white sunlight outside. The two prisoners hung by their arms from a horizontal beam erected in front of the stone house. Their shirts had been stripped off, and their white skin burned. Both made valiant efforts to maintain consciousness. They tried to raise their heads despite their rapidly ebbing strength.

He knew the terrible pain they suffered as blood drained from their arms and their bones pulled from joints and sockets. These mercenaries, he thought, they act so proudly. For what? They were dying. They had hung there for several hours. And until he changed his mind, they would remain there.

"Their names are Lee Hatton and Alex Nanos. They are mercenaries."

"Yes, sir!" Once again, Banu's leader had done the impossible, knowing the names of the prisoners before they had even been questioned.

"I want to know everything. You will instruct my eyes and ears in Kinshasa and in the villages to bring me the information—when they arrived in Kinshasa, why they are here. Everything! And when I have that information, I will supervise their interrogation, but not before. Do you understand?"

"Yes, sir!"

The man at the window wheeled around, moving his whole body to turn his head. His eyes were in darkness, but light cast through the open shutters played across a slight smirk. "Remember, Commander Banu. The less I have to interrogate them, the more intact they remain, and if you do your job well, you shall have the woman to play with. Is that sufficient incentive?"

Banu smiled with sudden enthusiasm. "You are doing good to rely on me, sir, for I shall do as you have instructed."

"Good. Then you can also arrange for an accident to happen to the Land Rover. A fire would be good. And some charred corpses that cannot be identified. If anyone comes looking for the doctor or these two, their search must end. For it to end we must give them a logical conclusion. Do you understand?"

"I understand perfectly, sir."

"There is one last thing," the man by the window said. He stepped forward into the light to face the tall uniformed African.

A tremor of fear crossed Banu's face. It was not easy to quiet the instinctive terrors that had been ingrained in him as a child.

The boss indeed had no neck. His head was welded to his shoulders evenly around the line of his jaw and chin. Dark hair grew on top of his head, and a livid red welt marked the back and sides. But his eyes were more terrifying than the ugly scars or the deformed body. They were empty.

"Tell the scientists they are to meet here in half an hour. We are moving the schedule ahead by one week. That means you must have your men begin the blood collections in the villages almost immediately."

"Yes, sir!" Banu answered crisply. His voice wavered. "Sir, may I ask you why this is suddenly necessary?"

"A precaution, Commander. Nothing more. You are dismissed."

Lost in thought, he flicked the shutter closed as the African left the room, and stood for a while in darkness. Then he moved stiffly to the desk and adjusted the lampshade. The light fell across his face. He looked at his reflection in a gilt-framed mirror on the nearby wall. To shrug, to shake, to nod—it was all impossible with his head frozen to his shoulders like a plastic doll or a comic-book monster.

The scarred white skin on the back of his head was shiny, vividly outlining the red serrations where hundreds of stitches had been removed, along with the vertebrae that had once made up his neck. He had been lucky to survive—five bullets pumped into the back of his head and buried alive in an Ethiopian death pit. Barrabas was not the only man with nine lives.

A dull ache of momentary anxiety in the pit of his stomach caught him off guard. What if Barrabas had survived? he thought. To all but him, the idea was impossible. And why were those two mercs prowling in his backyard? Were the other SOBs somewhere in Zaire? Had they got word to the outside world?

The course that had been charted, however, was irrevocable. There were the nameless masters who had plotted and financed it. To them he was responsible, and any failure would likely result in his own elimination. It was vitally important to tie up the two loose ends—to be neat, precise, exhaustive. The odds were with him.

No one could stop the most virulent plague of the twentieth century from sweeping through the human populations of the northern hemisphere. And no one could stop him from having what was his. Erika Dykstra.

## 7

Walker "The Fixer" Jessup leaned his enormous weight back in his cushioned chair and surveyed Manhattan through the rain. Beyond the plate-glass wall of his forty-second-floor office, the towers of New York's fabled skyline were little more than texture, gray on gray.

Jessup belched. With his left hand he pushed his lunch plate and cutlery to the side of his desk. He cast a baleful eye at the vista of open cracker packages and crumbs littered across the shiny desktop. A ten-litre vat of Russian caviar was open at his right elbow. Fish eggs. All the way from Moscow.

Suddenly he felt nauseous. Lunch had been an orgy of indulgence, beginning shortly after he had arrived at his office that morning and discovered that the shipment from Erika Dykstra had arrived. He'd come up for air four hours and several quarts of caviar later.

Would Barrabas ever forgive him for revealing his whereabouts to his ex-girlfriend? An indiscretion perhaps, but surely a small one. Erika's bribe was irresistible. Walker Jessup's weakness for delicacies was exceeded only by gluttony, and the size of his gut. He was so big, he couldn't get close to his desk, and he always found himself stretching to answer the phone or sign letters or grab a seventh helping.

A diet. He needed to go on a diet. He sighed hopelessly, catching a pungent whiff of Lake Baikal sturgeon, heavy on the air. His stomach rolled. He had definitely had his fill. With a broad sweep of his right arm, crackers, packages, caviar and his paper plate disappeared over the side of the desk into the deluxe-model Destroy It paper-shredder. Sensors triggered the automatic activator. Metal teeth gnashed, wheels churned, and a moment later an unappetizing puree gushed and dribbled out of the other side and into the trash can.

Sometimes the big Texan wondered how he had been reduced to such a state. Was it fifteen harrowing years as a CIA operative before going into private business as a "consultant"? Or was his steady compulsion to eat a self-destructive guilt impulse, a self-inflicted punishment for all the cold hard cash that came across his desk each time he signed away a Third World government, or manufactured a scandal to eliminate unfavored opposition leaders in a banana republic?

They didn't call him the Fixer for nothing, he thought proudly. And with a touch of contrition, he warned himself, Walker Jessup, you're fixin' to have a massive coronary.

A short beep from his telephone alerted him that the answering service had received a message. With considerable difficulty, he stretched forward to pick up the receiver. It seemed farther away than it had several hours earlier. He belched again, his mouth filling with the taste of half-digested Russian sturgeon off-spring. It was disgusting. Never again, he vowed. And a smaller voice asked weakly, will Barrabas ever forgive me?

He pushed the asterisk on the telephone, which instantly connected him to the service. A man answered. Enough telephones were ringing in the background to make it sound like an evangelical pledge center. The answering-service operator was vague.

"Uh, yeah, somewhere here, I just had it. Oh yeah, here it is. Someone from, uh, I dunno, the Missionary Service or something had a message from someone about something somewhere in Africa. Lemme see, I can't read my own writing sometimes. Oh yeah, Les Haddon? Is that it? You know a Les Haddon?"

Jessup ran through his mental Rolodex. "Lee Hatton?" he ventured, a sharpened pencil poised over a scratch pad.

"Oh, yeah! That's it! I think. Anyway, there's a message for you to call Cody Yellow, and, uh, they left a number. It's in Africa or someplace, uh, it's kinda weird. Three dash fifty-six, twenty-eight dash thirty-three. No area code, but they'll be in touch later."

Jessup hung up. He had ten cases of caviar left in the outside office, and he was going to personally stuff every one of them down the throat of the answering-service operator. He swivelled his chair to the left to face a small computer monitor.

He was familiar with the Missionary Network from his CIA days. It was not uncommon for the well-meaning Christians who ran it to unwittingly convey top-secret intelligence messages. The so-called phone number was obviously location coordinates. He rapidly typed them into the computer. The screen flashed and came up with a map of Zaire. Of course! Jessup snapped his fingers. Lee and Alex had gone there for a few weeks to work with some researchers on an AIDS project. But code yellow was serious biz. The mercs wouldn't use it without a damned good reason.

He picked up the phone and called the Cairo hotel where Barrabas was registered. The line buzzed and crackled across the Atlantic, over the Mediterranean and up the Nile.

*"Non, monsieur,"* the Egyptian voice answered in accented French. "Monsieur Barrabas checked out several days ago. No, monsieur, he left no forwarding address. *Non, monsieur*, I did not actually see him leave myself. He sent someone to pick up his luggage. I am glad to be of help, *monsieur*."

Walker Jessup could feel the caviar in his stomach sinking like sludge to the bottom of Lake Baikal. Barrabas never went anywhere without letting the Fixer know. It was one of the rules.

He thought a moment, picked up the phone and placed a call to Amsterdam. The maid answered.

*"Goedendag! Nee, Mevrouw Dykstra is niet hier. Nee*, she left yesterday in a great hurry. Gunter was in a terrible accident, *mijnheer. Ja*, she left immediately. He is in hospital. He has been shot. *Nee, niet in Amsterdam, mijnheer*. In Egypt. Cairo, Egypt."

She gave Jessup the name of the hotel before hanging up. The caviar in his stomach was transmuting, gaining molecular weight by the minute. It was turning to lead. He called Cairo again.

"*Non, monsieur*, Madame Dykstra checked out this morning. To Kinshasa, I believe. I am glad to be of help, *monsieur*."

Jessup slammed down the telephone receiver, his hand frozen to it and his knuckles white. He had a feeling he shouldn't have told Erika that Nile Barrabas was in Cairo. What had happened to Gunter? What in hell was going on? This was no code yellow. It was a green, for go.

He pushed his vast weight up from his chair with considerable difficulty and lumbered to a wall safe hidden behind some bookshelves on the far wall. The list he removed was updated when necessary.

Claude Hayes, the guerrilla warfare expert, was out in California indulging his favorite pastime—deep-sea fishing.

What in hell was Nate Beck, the team's computer and electronics genius, doing in Indianapolis?

Billy Two, the whacked-out Osage survivalist and tracker, was lost in the Arizona desert again, chasing after one of his native Indian spiritual visions. Scratch that cat.

Liam O'Toole, the SOBs' demolitions man had listed the number of his Greenwich Village apartment. His expertise extended to demolishing his own life. He was probably three sheets to the wind—if the booze hadn't already made him pass out.

Jessup sank heavily into his chair with a groan of desperation. Life was cruel, and Barrabas would never forgive him. Ten cases of caviar in the outer office: in very short order he was going to punish himself severely.

He picked up the phone and started punching out numbers.

NATE BECK SAW THE OPENING and pressed the accelerator to the floor. Unleashed, the three-wheeled Trihawk Star II ate velocity like a starved greyhound. In the bottom of his eye he saw the digital speedometer climb from 138 to the maximum speed of 145. Seven extra miles an hour did it. He left the twin Cortinos eating dust and climbed abreast of the DAC Leopard 101.

The flagman whipped his arm down, marking off the seventy-third lap. There were two more to go, and all he had to do was leave the Leopard chewing his tail pipes to win the Indianapolis racetrack's hundred-thousand-dollar pot.

The Trihawk was the prototype of a new three-wheeled racing car designed and built by Dorian Maran. The boys in the pit had laughed when they had wheeled it off the truck.

"Start crying," Nate muttered between clenched teeth. Knowing an opportunity when it looked him in the face, Dorian had bet a thousand dollars on the spot. By the time the man with the clipboard had made the rounds of owners and mechanics, it was up to forty. And that was just the pit. There was a helluva lot riding on Nate's first semiprofessional race.

Car racing had been a long-standing passion, but one the computer wizard had rarely had time to indulge. For years there had been his time-consuming work designing codes for the U.S. Army and later heading the R&D division of a major electronics corporation when most people thought "chips" were made from potatoes. Then there had been his wife, Barbara or Beverley or something—he liked to forget.

Nate Beck had spent the first thirty years of his life mired in drudgery and spending his preferred time in an action/adventure fantasy world. One day he had decided to step over the line. He had used a computer scheme to rip off a million dollars in nickels and dimes from bank accounts and had fled to Switzerland.

His wife had ratted. He owed her for it. A guy named Nile Barrabas had snapped him up minutes before Interpol had arrived. The line he had stepped over was the frontier of a land where dreams come true. When the SOBs were on assignment, he spent a lot more time behind a computer console than an M-60, but the life agreed with him.

And made him rich—rich enough to become one of Dorian Maran's major backers. And confident enough that when the brilliant racing car designer had needed a driver for the experimental prototype, Beck had asked for an immediate return on his money. He was the perfect size for it—slim and on the short side of medium height. What he lacked in experience he made up in guts. The risks he faced on the Indianapolis racetrack were minuscule compared to an average job with the Soldiers of Barrabas. The Trihawk eased forward, pushing half a car length ahead of the Leopard, and loosing it on a curve. He cursed himself for slowing as he went into it, and put it down to inexpe-

rience. But the driver of the Leopard took advantage
of his momentary lead to pull over, cutting Beck off
and forcing him to slow further to avoid hitting a
concrete barrier.

Now it was time to show the folks what the Trihawk was all about. Beck snarled, wrenching the
steering wheel full circle to the right. The turn would
have toppled any other car at that speed. The three-
wheeled Trihawk angled sideways behind the DAC
Leopard. Beck straightened it, floored again, and the
prototype inched ahead of the Leopard just as they
passed the pit.

He gasped, hesitated a tenth of a second—long
enough for the Leopard to take the initiative and crawl
past his front fender. Damned if Claude Hayes wasn't
standing there beside Dorian Maran, arms on hips,
and watching him go around. There was only one imperative that would make Claude give up a fishing trip.

The Leopard pissed him off. He squeezed his foot
against the accelerator pedal and twisted the wheel to
the left. His tires came within fractions of an inch of
his opponent. The crowd roared. The DAC driver
backed off. It was enough. Half a minute later the
flagman brought his arm down, the spectators in the
sold out grandstand rose unanimously to their feet,
and Nate Beck won his first race. He braked in front
of the pit stop where the air was thick with the odors
of gas and burnt rubber.

"Hey, man! Man! Man!" Dorian Maran was a
short thin man with blond hair and an eagerness that
belied his usual cool. He ran to the Trihawk as Beck
stepped out and pulled off his goggles. The mechan-

ics on Maran's team swept forward to congratulate him. "Man, we have just made one hundred and forty thou—"

Beck put his arms out and strode past them, practically running toward the tall, muscular black man standing by the pumps. He moved past him into the dressing rooms, unzipping his silver Mylar suit. Hayes followed.

"What in hell, Claude," Beck shouted over the deafening roar of the cars still finishing their laps on the track.

"People missing all over the place, and Jessup's throwing a shit fit," Hayes said calmly.

Beck tugged the flashy togs off his shoulders, stepping quickly from the pant legs.

"Where to?" he asked, grabbing a leather jacket from his locker.

"The heart of the Dark Continent. Kinshasa."

"Formerly Léopoldville. In Zaire, formerly the Belgian Congo. Know the place?"

Hayes forced a smile as the two men walked toward the door with the exit sign. "S'like hometown to me."

**8**

Brazzaville and Kinshasa were twin cities, squatting on the northern and southern banks of the broad and muddy Congo at the beginning of the great delta. The legendary river, its branches and tributaries, snaked through swamps and steaming rain forests, emptying into the South Atlantic Ocean two hundred miles to the west.

Erika Dykstra looked down at the river-veined jungles as her Air Africa flight descended for its approach to Ndolo Airport on the outskirts of Kinshasa. From the air, the city looked modern. There were long, straight streets with boulevards in the European style, an old quarter of nineteenth-century apartment buildings built by the Belgian colonialists. The down town consisted of dozens of shabby modern office buildings.

Instead of suburbs on its outskirts, the teeming metropolis gave way to shanty towns, where corrugated tin roofs gleamed in the afternoon sun. Beyond, small villages of thatched stick and mud houses built around cattle-filled kraals were scattered like pebbles across the baked and brittle land.

A flight attendant leaned over Erika Dykstra's seat. "*Madam*, have you been to Kinshasa before?"

The Dutch woman shook her head.

"We usually warn people that it's a very big city—more than three million people—and very dirty. We advise our passengers that when they go out they should not wear watches, jewelry or carry handbags." Her eyes fell, lighting on Erika's gold necklace and rings, before she moved on to the next seat.

The air closed around the Dutch woman like a steam bath the moment she stepped from the airplane onto the ramp. By the time she crossed the runway to the terminal building, her cotton dress was soaking wet, the handles of her shoulder bag slippery.

The airport was a zoo. Wandering tribes of missionaries rushed to catch outbound flights to Europe, while herds of tourists safari bound and clad in khaki scurried for taxis. Fat government bureaucrats in expensive suits organized their numerous wives who were wearing brightly colored *kangas* and their little children rolled across the white tile floors like plump chocolate-covered raisins. From overhead speakers a burry voice rhymed off the names of their destinations: Lagos, Lusaka, Nairobi, Harare, Addis Ababa and Dar es Salaam, capitals of the modern African republics.

Erika fought her way to passport control. Dozens of hands clutching passports flailed in the air in front of a single narrow window. A lone Zairian functionary sat on a stool with a rubber stamp. Suddenly a small black man in an old-fashioned suit blocked her way.

"Your passport, please," he said smoothly, extending an arm.

With a reluctance born of suspicion, Erika handed over the valuable document. To her surprise, the man reappeared a moment later with the required stamp and additional papers to fill out.

"State the amount of currency you have brought with you and give these papers to the officer when you go through customs. I must warn you, do not exchange money on the parallel market." His broad smile revealed a single gold tooth. "And I suggest you pick up your baggage immediately before it is stolen off the conveyer belt." He bowed graciously as she passed. "Enjoy your visit to Zaire!"

Customs consisted of a series of wooden tables manned by overweight soldiers. The ones with the most stripes lounged carelessly, using the tabletops for seats. Their ample rear ends threatened to crack the slender legs. Several of them stood and eyed the pretty blond woman as she approached, nudging each other and winking.

Two of them opened her suitcase and pawed through her clothing.

"Business?" one asked grimly, prying open the cosmetics compartment.

"I'm a tourist. And I'm in a hurry, if you know what I mean." She handed him her passport, with five hundred crisp new zaires folded in the documents she had just filled out. The customs guard was filled with happiness.

"Welcome to Zaire!"

She was in. And so was her gun.

The madhouse continued on the sidewalks outside. A fleet of oddly shaped yellow vehicles lined the curbs, taxi drivers shouting and calling for fares, while prospective customers fought over them.

"Kinshasa, lady!" A tall thin man with a wiry black moustache took her by the elbow and propelled her into the back seat of his taxi.

"The King Leopold Hotel," she instructed. He tore off into the traffic heading from the airport into the city.

Now she saw Africa, teeming beyond her open window. The tall black women, walking erect with jars and baskets balanced carefully on their heads, the children herding starved, emaciated cattle, men carrying great clusters of red bananas.

Her driver drove into the city along the broad central avenue named after the date of the Zairian revolution. The hotel was a remnant of colonial days, a stone beaux art edifice that might have been imported from the streets of Paris or Brussels. By reputation it was still the most efficient hotel in the city.

By the time she had registered, supervised the flock of bellboys, all of whom wanted to carry her two suitcases to her room, and cleared the cockroaches away from the bed by flicking them with a towel, she thought of nothing but a long, soapy bath.

Brown water trickled slowly from the ancient tap and formed a ring of ocher sediment in the bottom of the old-fashioned tub. She sat on the porcelain edge, staring at it for a few minutes and wondering what to do next. Then she burst into tears.

After a few moments she fought it, sniffled and wiped the tears away with a towel. Inhaling deeply to make herself feel efficient, she got up and walked back into the bedroom, where her suitcase lay on a stool near the dresser. She flung open the lid, and withdrew a photograph of Nile Barrabas from between the folds of her clothing. Then she burrowed into the cosmetics compartment, lifted the false bottom and took out the gun.

She knew she was serious when a gun made her feel better. Once again she opened the mag to look at the bullets. The vision of her brother, silent, swathed in bandages, supine in an iron bed in an Egyptian hospital, swam painfully before her eyes.

There was a knock on the door.

She put the gun in her shoulder bag.

"Just a moment," she called. Quickly she swept her cosmetics back into the suitcase and closed it. Then she checked herself in the mirror. To her own surprise, she looked perfectly calm. She opened the door.

A tall dark man wearing a long white gown and a small skull-cap waved at her with a toothy smile. "I am Ahmed. Your driver."

She looked at him for a moment, trying to figure out what he was talking about. Finally it clicked.

"I didn't order a driver," she said.

"Not yet, *madame*. But I am best driver in Kinshasa. Very good price for European lady."

"Just a moment." She closed the door and dialed the desk on the telephone by her bed. The clerk assured her that Ahmed was indeed considered the best driver in Kinshasa.

"Forgive me, *madame*. I took 'ze liberty of zending him to your room on the assumption you would want one. 'Zere iz no obligation of course. My deepest apologies for 'ze disturb—"

"No, no, that's quite all right. I'm in Kinshasa to find someone. I have a photograph. I'd like you to look at it. Perhaps he was a guest here. Then I'll decide if I need a driver. It will be worth your time."

A few moments later the desk manager was at her room. Ahmed gave a deferential nod of his head and waited politely outside the door.

Erika showed him the photograph.

"Ah, zis man, *oui, madame*! 'E was a guest here but left for 'ze interior several days ago. 'E is your 'usband, a friend...?"

"A long-lost cousin." She took a thousand zaires from her wallet and shuffled the big paper notes noisily. "You don't happen to know where he went do you?"

The desk manager eyed the money. "But of course. He went to Isipo. It is in 'ze eastern sector, near 'ze frontier."

Erika moved the money closer to him, then stopped. "And how would someone travel quickly to Isipo?"

His eyes glanced at hers and returned to the money. "'Zere is a zingle paved road in Zaire, *madame*, and it runs eight hundred miles east to 'ze frontier. It iz a town, not far from 'ze end."

"I see. And with this driver, I suppose."

The desk manager shrugged. "Twice a week 'zere is an airplane, but I think not for four more days."

Erika smiled and handed him half the money. He smiled back. His hand remained poised in front of him, waiting for the rest of it.

"And should any further information concerning this...Nile Barrabas...come your way—" Erika laid the zaires on top of the others and held on "—you'll be sure to inform me."

"It would be a playzure, *madame*." The desk manager bowed slightly and turned for the door.

She smiled and let go.

"Tell Ahmed he's hired. I want him to take me to the airport tomorrow morning. That's as far as I go for now."

"Certainly, *madame*. Whatever your wish may be."

When the desk manager had gone, Erika walked slowly to the window. Dusk was falling over the Zairian capital, and the city had slowed, weary from the heat and toil of the equatorial day. The people living on the street lit small fires at the curbs, preparing to cook whatever scraps they had scavenged during the day. Mothers folded sheets of cardboard into mattresses for their children to sleep on. This, too, was Africa, the dire poverty, the desperate need.

Erika shivered despite the fading heat. She felt alone.

A taxi slowed in front of the King Leopold Hotel's porte cochere just as the old iron streetlamps came to life, tinting the darkening night a friendly yellow. The door of the taxi opened, and two men got out. The driver opened the trunk and handed them their luggage. Duffel bags. One of them tipped the driver. They picked up their bags and headed up the steps of the hotel.

In the west the sun was a great neon ball, perfectly round, rippling through waves of purple heat as it descended rapidly to the steaming horizon. For a moment the air moved, almost a breeze.

Erika's breath caught in her throat, and something clawed inside her, trapped, fighting for air. She forced it aside and watched. She knew those men.

She turned into the room, eyeing her handbag, aware of the gun inside it. Then she picked up the telephone.

"The desk manager, please. Hello, it's Miss Dykstra again. I want you to do me another favor. Concerning those two men checking in. Yes. Claude Hayes and Nate Beck. I'll make it worth your while."

NATE BECK SQUINTED against the bright early-morning sun as he and Claude Hayes trotted down the steps of the King Leopold Hotel the next morning. They were on the trail of Nile Barrabas, Lee Hatton and Alex Nanos, and their first rendezvous was at Mama Yemu Hospital.

According to Jessup's research, someone there would know where Lee Hatton was—or was supposed to be. The woman merc had failed to report after the first message had been relayed to Jessup, and the Fixer had grown more and more frantic by the minute. It had been a relief for both men when they had boarded the jet at JFK and were rid of him.

Barrabas's disappearance was even more puzzling. There was no reason Jessup knew of for him to come to Kinshasa, and it was unlikely that he knew Lee Hatton was there. Then there was the matter of the Dykstras. Erika had disappeared from her home in Amsterdam, and a call to six Cairo hospitals had finally yielded a confirmation that Gunter had been wounded and was still in a coma.

All in all, it added up to trouble.

A Zairian with grizzled white hair opened his eyes and looked up from the wheel of his taxi, decided they didn't need him and slumped over the steering wheel again. Up and down the grand boulevard the street people kindled little fires at the curb—this time to cook breakfast. Older children washed their baby siblings in puddles of muddy water.

"It sure ain't Indy," Nate cracked with a wry smile.

"Bad joke, man," Claude Hayes said humorlessly.

"What do you mean?"

"Just take it from me. Come on, let's walk."

The two men had barely taken three steps when Hayes stopped.

"Hey, Nate. I'm sorry. Sometimes I get real serious and loose my sense of humor."

Beck put his hands up and shook his head. "Uh-uh, Claude. It was my mistake." He looked up and down the street at the incredible poverty. The street people went about their morning rituals of washing and eating. Some had begun to fold up their little campsites before crowds of pedestrians poured into Kinshasa's central core and trampled them into dust.

"I'll tell you. More people from Indy ought to come here and see this."

The black merc slapped him on the back. "Forget it. It's one of the worst experiences in the world, seeing this kind of poverty and knowing that whatever you do is like bailing out floodwaters with a teaspoon. Everyone handles it their own way. We got half an hour to kill, and the hospital's down this way. Let's pass on a taxi and see the sights."

"You really do know your way around Kinshasa!" Nate teased.

"Hey, I told you. It's like hometown to me. Back in the days—not so long ago—when Zimbabwe was still called Rhodesia, and Angola was under Portuguese control, we used to organize the guerrilla strategy sessions here. The Zairians kicked out the Belgians in the early sixties, so Kinshasa was the closest safe place to trouble."

Hayes rarely talked about his past, especially the years after he left the U.S. Navy SEALs and fought as a guerrilla leader in the liberation wars in Africa. The black man was deeply committed to the struggles of his people for equality. Sometimes, when it got bad enough, someone had to do it with a gun.

"Man, that's why I left I guess," Hayes continued. "I put in my years fighting for the cause. I'm glad I did, and I think everyone should...you know, do something for charity. I'm a soldier, so that's what I gave. But you can only do so much, then you're burned out, and you gotta pass the torch. I still come back, though. I like to come back."

"How come?"

"Because it's my history, Nate. It's part of me as a black man. Same as Europe is for your Jewish ancestors."

"Biggest group of hustlers, swindlers and scam artists to come out of the Polish ghettos," the New York native said wistfully. "You know, Claude, something's been bothering me since last night. You know when we asked the desk manager if the colonel had been registered, and you showed him the photo to jar his memory?"

"Yeah. And he said no go. Even the tip didn't help."

"Yeah. Just like that. He was convinced. But he didn't even look at the picture. Not really. I think he was hiding something."

Hayes nodded. "So what are you suggesting?"

"Nothing. Just thought I'd point it out."

The mercs turned off the tree-lined boulevard onto a shopping street, where East Indian and Asian merchants pushed up the metal grilles of their shops and scrawny dogs missing great blotches of fur pawed through garbage in the gutters. The streets were filling with traffic. Hundreds of strange contraptions had been assembled from bits and pieces of other vehicles and somehow glued to noisy internal combustion engines that belched clouds of sooty black smoke.

A few minutes later they passed into quieter streets. A whitewashed wall ran along the sidewalk on one side. Zaire's biggest hospital sprawled behind it, a mishmash of buildings, modern and ancient. Entrance was gained through a high wrought-iron gate. It was guarded by soldiers with automatic rifles. A crowd of women holding sick children jostled and seethed, begging entrance, each one pleading for her child to be treated.

Nate and Hayes showed their passports, with Hayes explaining in Swahili that they had an appointment to see Dr. Nzila. The soldiers opened the gate. Nate closed his eyes in sorrow as the mob of desperate mothers backed out of their way in dull leaden silence. The two mercs pushed into the compound.

They wandered from building to building in search of the office number they were given. Africans washed their clothing and one another in the courtyards between the long barracks-like buildings that served as wards. Finally they found the office off a crowded corridor lined with stretchers. A nurse wheeled a man past them and parked him outside Dr. Nzila's door. His face was swollen so badly that his eyes, nose and mouth had been forced closed, and tubes fed oxygen into his nostrils from a portable tank. A deep red sore covered his forehead. Only the labored rise and fall of his chest indicated he was alive.

Hayes raised his hand to knock when the door opened, and a tall black man in a white lab coat stood before them. He held a clipboard and flipped through pages of notes and charts.

"Ah, Mr. Hayes. Go in and sit. I'll be right back." Dr.Nzila rushed past them, stopping momentarily to look at the patient on the stretcher, before disappearing down the crowded corridor.

The mercs went inside and sat in small wooden chairs beside a scarred wooden desk littered with work papers. Hayes nudged Beck and pointed to the blackboard on the wall behind it. In chalk the words "AIDS—Confirmed" had been scrawled, and underneath there were dates and numbers.

"More than doubling, every six months," he said.

"Those figures are meaningless," Dr. Nzila's voice boomed from the doorway. The Zairian entered, shaking hands with each of the mercs. He scarcely looked at them as he moved to his desk, shuffling through papers and making check marks on his clipboard with a pencil.

"In the interior of the country there are perhaps tens of thousands of cases. The man outside the door, for example. The lesion on his face was nothing more than a cold sore—but one that has blinded him and eaten through his skull to his brain. But that is only one of many diseases. Here in Africa, malaria and tuberculosis are common—like the mumps or chicken pox in America. Most Africans who live to be older than two years are immune to them. Until recently. Suddenly people are dying of them, and other things as well. We don't know when it will stop. Here in Zaire, it has another name. The Horror. Forgive my haste today, gentlemen, but I was presented with a certain crisis when I arrived for work this morning. You are friends of Dr. Hatton, I believe. How may I help you?"

The story Hayes told him had been carefully prepared in advance. "We're working with the Boston team of researchers on the AIDS project and came to assist Dr. Hatton in her fieldwork. Unfortunately we've had difficulty contacting her—"

Dr. Nzila slapped his clipboard down and leaned forward over his cluttered desk.

"Dr. Hatton and her assistant, a man named—" he shuffled through the papers on his clipboard until he came to it "—Alex Nanos, accompanied the regional health officer on a fact-finding tour into the jungles east of a small town called Isipo. I'm afraid it will be impossible to contact her. I suggest you gentlemen return to your hotel and wait for her to contact you. Now, if you don't mind . . ."

Nzila strode from behind his desk and opened the door for them. The noisy bustle from the hospital corridor flooded the room. Beck stood, looking uncertainly from Hayes to the Zairian doctor. Hayes lolled back in his chair and stretched his legs, not bothering to turn around as he spoke.

"I also bring greetings from the Fixer. He wants to thank you for the input on the Angolan situation."

Dr. Nzila paused, considering his options for a moment. He closed his office door.

"You may convey my respectful greetings to Mr. Jessup. I was glad to be of help. However, it would be best that my assistance wasn't mentioned out loud in this country. My government is a close ally of the Angolan government and might not approve of my cooperation. Now what can I do for you?"

Hayes turned around and faced him.

"We have to find Hatton and Nanos. Now. Today."

"That could be difficult." Nzila walked slowly around them and sat at his desk, his face clouded with impending defeat.

"There has been an uprising in the towns along the eastern frontier. Villagers and tribesmen have at-

tacked and burned the Croix Rouge and mission hospitals alike, dragging out doctors and nurses and
hacking them to pieces. Apparently they have been
urged on by some of the local witch doctors, and the
flames of their panic have been fanned by the rapid
spread of the Horror. A platoon of army regulars was
sent to quell the uprising. The officers and loyal soldiers were killed and those who survived have apparently joined forces with the mob.''

"And Isipo?''

"Isipo so far has not been touched, and more army
units are being rushed to the area. Unfortunately, Dr.
Obispo left the hospital there several days ago with
Dr.Hatton and this man Nanos. They have not been
heard from since.''

The mercs threw each other looks of growing dread.

"How do we get there?'' Beck asked.

"Normally by air twice a week. But the military has
cancelled all unauthorized flights to the region. There
is a road, a single road that runs eight hundred miles
to the east. It is paved. Sort of.'' Dr. Nzila hesitated,
studying the two men cautiously. He chose his next
words carefully. "I assume from your friendship with
Walker Jessup that you both have an expertise in areas
other than medicine.''

"You might put it that way,'' Hayes replied, eyeing
the Zairian doctor steadily. The Fixer had arranged for
a Peruvian diplomat to carry their automatic rifles and
ammunition through Ndolo airport.

Nzila paused a moment, then continued. "I have a
Jeep and driver leaving in two hours. It is a two-day
journey, but I am determined to see the situation for

myself. It may be extremely dangerous. With that in mind, I would be pleased to have two competent men accompanying me, and I invite you.''

Hayes stood. ''At the King Leopold Hotel. In two hours. We'll be ready.''

''Anything in particular we should bring?'' Nate asked, leaving his chair and following Hayes to the door.

Nzila nodded. ''Guns.'' He turned back to the papers on his desk.

## 9

Erika Dykstra emerged from the battered yellow taxi on a desolate airstrip somewhere outside Kinshasa. Clouds of yellow dust scudded along the baked earth, swept by hot breezes. The humidity remained unchanged. The air was thick enough to float on.

She told Ahmed to wait at the car and strode past a line of derelict small planes, their mechanical innards hanging from their bellies, cannibalized for spare parts. Of five shabby hangars, paint peeling and doors falling from hinges, one looked like it was still used.

Inside the dim building, a black man in mechanic's overalls shouted and cursed, doing a small dance around an airplane and waving pliers in the air. Spread on the dirt floor were thousands of nuts, washers, gadgets and other bits and pieces of engine.

Three Zairians, younger but covered equally with engine grease, stood on the sidelines and watched impassively as the mechanic shrieked in anger and kicked at the earth, scattering parts in all directions. When they saw the European woman at the door, they turned coolly away, diverting themselves at the workbench along the back wall.

The Zairian in the blue overalls stopped his strange dance and looked wide-eyed at the woman standing uncertainly at his door. Erika walked in, wary of another strange outburst and the tool still in the mechanic's hands.

"What can I do, lady?" the man shouted, seemingly in exasperation. He threw his hands into the air. Erika wasn't sure if he was asking about the repair job in front of him or trying to be helpful.

"I'm looking for Mbuji Shabongo." The name had been given to her by the helpful desk manager at the King Leopold Hotel. He was earning his money. A lot of it, too.

"That be me, lady. What you want?"

"I want to go to Isipo."

"Next plane go in four days." The man turned around and walked back toward the broken-down airplane, obviously finished with her.

"I want to hire a bush pilot privately to take me there."

Mbuji turned again and waved his hands at her, shooing her away. "No can do that, lady. Army come. Take all private planes for emergency. Come back another day."

"But I was told you were a bush pilot. I'll pay. Quite well, too."

The black man threw his head back and clutched his belly. His laughter pealed through the airy high-roofed hangar. When he finished, he looked at her, tears of mirth streaming down his cheeks.

It must have been funny, Erika thought. Mbuji could barely talk. He squeezed the words out between teeth and giggles and pointed to the airplane. "You fix, I fly." Like lightning striking, he flew into a rage again, shouting and cursing in his African dialect, kicking clouds of dust and engine parts into the air.

Erika looked at the situation, powerless to change it, and she felt a growing sense of desperation. She wanted to get to Barrabas first, and the only way to do it was by airplane. To top it all off, there was this mysterious emergency in the eastern provinces. The desk manager had whispered rumors of it to her before she'd set out that morning. Now it looked serious. There was no doubt in her mind that somehow Barrabas was involved.

She turned to storm back to the taxi and ran head on into Ahmed, who had been standing several feet behind her. She glared, angry that he hadn't waited at the car. He beamed on, oblivious to her anger.

"I take you to Isipo. We drive. I best driver in Kinshasa."

"How did you know I wanted to go to Isipo?" Erika demanded.

"I hear you say. We drive. Two thousand zaires."

Erika wasn't listening. She stomped across the desolate airstrip toward the taxi. Ahmed ran hastily after her, his solicitous smile still pasted across his face.

Half an hour later Ahmed pulled the car up in front of the King Leopold Hotel. Erika leaned forward from the rear seat and jerked his shoulder.

"Quick. Go past and pull over there," she ordered, gesturing to the next street corner. Mystified but obliging, Ahmed did as he was instructed.

Erika turned around to look out the rear window. Claude Hayes and Nate Beck were standing on the steps of the hotel, talking to a black man who had just emerged from the back of an open Jeep. The driver remained at the wheel as the three men turned and went back into the hotel.

"Ahmed," Erika called, fishing through her shoulder bag for more of the red paper zaires. "A tip. But only if you do exactly as I say. I want you to go over to the driver of the Jeep back there and be friendly to him."

"Friendly?" Ahmed was genuinely puzzled.

"Yes. Just chat with him. Find out where he's taking those men. But I don't want them to know, do you understand?"

Ahmed's face lit up and he nodded. "I understand very good, *madame*. One taxi driver talking to another about the boss. Four hundred zaires."

"Two hundred. And two hundred more if I get the information."

Ahmed nodded. Erika handed him the notes. She shrunk down in the seat to be invisible. Ahmed drove around the block and parked behind the Jeep. Then he left the taxi and lit a cigarette, looking at the sky and watching the smoke curl up from his mouth to prove how bored he was. Occasionally he glanced at the driver of the Jeep. Eventually they made eye contact. Ahmed smiled.

He wandered over to the other driver, offered a cigarette and complained about the stupid *mzungu* who had so much money that they threw it everywhere without realizing how much it was worth. The other driver agreed. They discussed it for a long time until the black doctor and his two guests emerged from the hotel and threw their duffel bags into the rear of the Jeep. Ahmed nodded goodbye to the driver. The Jeep pulled out as he slipped back into his yellow taxi.

"What did he say?"

"They go to Isipo," Ahmed said, beaming as usual. It made sense to him.

Erika handed him another two hundred zaires. There was one other way to track down Barrabas. Follow the leader.

"Ahmed, how long will it take?"

The driver held up two fingers. "Eight hundred miles. I have extra gas in trunk. Two days."

"You're hired. I want to get my luggage from my room. Can you help me carry it down?"

Ahmed was glad to be of assistance. Erika asked for her bill at the desk and was assured by the manager once again that Ahmed was an excellent driver and that she was in good hands. She nodded absentmindedly and handed over another handful of paper zaires. Ahmed followed her to her room. Her suitcase was already packed, sitting on the bed.

"There's another one in the bathroom," she told him. "Can you get it."

As soon as the taxi driver was inside, Erika slammed the door behind him and quickly locked it. Ahmed shouted in surprise. She withdrew the key and put it on the dresser. The driver's excited voice was muffled behind the thick wood panels. He called to her, unsure if it was a strange joke.

When she gave no answer, he started banging. The door expanded slightly with a loud thump as his weight fell against it. Erika wedged a wooden chair under the door handle. She grabbed her suitcase and fled.

A few minutes later Erika Dykstra was at the wheel of Ahmed's battered taxi, zipping down Kinshasa's broad tree-lined boulevard. She headed east into the dark equatorial rain forests of Africa's heartland.

THE JEEP CARRYING Nate Beck and Claude Hayes, along with the Zairian doctor, traveled easily for the first few hours beyond Kinshasa. The road was rutted, bumpy and cracked and the men jolted up and down as the Jeep lurched over potholes. They made good time, however, as the highway passed from dusty marginal farmland near the city, across great swamps, past seas of wavering, head-high elephant grass and into tangles of gigantic rain forest vegetation.

The road deteriorated noticeably after the first hundred miles. By late afternoon they had covered almost half of the distance to Isipo, but progress slowed considerably as the driver veered sharply and suddenly every few seconds to avoid another gap in the pavement or to detour around small pools whose bottoms were concealed by dirty water.

In the course of the afternoon they passed a variety of vehicles, ranging from sleek BMWs belonging to government officials, to ancient pickup trucks that looked like assembled pieces of jigsaw puzzles. But by far the majority of the traffic was pedestrian. On some stretches near villages, long lines of women bore baskets of strange fruit, and herdsmen urged accommodating herds of lyre-horned cattle down the middle of the road.

Other long stretches of the tattered highway were deserted and silent. Even the thick green jungles appeared eerily abandoned, empty except for occasional plaintive squawks from monkeys hidden in the foliage.

As the shadows of the trees grew long across the road, silhouetted by the deep lemon light of late afternoon, a wind came up, blowing dust into the air. The Zairians traveling on foot quickly disappeared into clouds of fine yellow powder, and the sky darkened further with ominous storm clouds in the east. They stopped, quickly snapping canvas panels into place on the sides of the Jeep to protect them from the oncoming deluge. A few moments later they drove into a wall of water so thick it was impossible to see past the front bumper. It thinned, and the driver pushed on as the shattering noise on the roof began to fade. Suddenly pieces of asphalt at the edge of the highway crumbled and dissolved under the wheels. Pebbles and chunks of tar swirled away in the fast-moving eddies. The storm moved on, disappearing as rapidly as it had approached.

The driver and Dr. Nzila consulted in rapid Swahili.

"He knows a place not far from here where we can pitch a tent for the night," the Zairian doctor told the two mercs. "It will rain off and on, and at night the highway becomes more treacherous."

Hayes agreed. "This Jeep is built tough, but one bad turn could leave us waiting for days for help."

Reluctantly Beck nodded. He was anxious to get to Isipo and find their comrades. There was little point, however, in jeopardizing the progress they had already made by pushing on blindly in the darkness and bad weather.

They found a clearing as the tropical night fell, blackness rolling in like a fog bank. They threw up the heavy canvas tent by the light from the high beams, hammering the steel pegs into sandy soil and weighting them with rocks to hold them down.

The forests around the clearing began to hum with swarms of mosquitoes, their numbers growing until a high-pitched hum stretched through the air like taut steel wire. Flying insects, so fat they seemed to have fed on growth hormones, tangled with their hands and clothing as they unfurled the guy ropes and stretched the canvas over the aluminum poles.

They had barely finished and crawled inside when distant thunder sounded, echoed and grew louder. Then something crashed through the forest, and another rain cloud burst. The marble-sized drops smashed into the canvas with such force that conversation was impossible. The storm moved on, leaving silence in its wake for a moment. Then, slowly at first but building quickly to a fevered pitch, the mosquitoes began anew, gnawing at night and sanity with the persistent humming drone of little wings.

"They seek blood," Dr. Nzila said. He lit a mosquito coil and set the smoking coal near the flaps at the front of the tent. "When I studied in America, I learned that they were considered only a minor nuisance, and the object of many jokes about vacations and camping trips. Here, they are bearers of doom—carrying dengue fever, elephantiasis, yellow fever, malaria. They are the servants of death.''

Morning came with a light fog, which burned away minutes after the big red African sun floated above the horizon. They brewed thick coffee over a Sterno can and chewed miserably on dried cereal. Nate disappeared in the foliage to relieve himself and returned seconds later, pale and excited.

''Biggest goddamn mother of a snake I've ever seen,'' he cried, pointing into the forest. Nzila and Hayes took the machete from the Jeep to explore. A few moments later they came back, laughing.

''Harmless,'' Hayes said. ''He just looked at us like royalty interrupted in a boudoir.''

''If it was any closer to lunchtime, we'd be eating him,'' Nzila promised, brandishing the machete.

''Eat the snake?'' Nate asked weakly.

The doctor nodded. ''Standard part of the diet here. The people are hungry. Are we ready?'' He looked over the loaded Jeep.

''If you want to take your constitutional...'' Hayes suggested to Nate.

The diminutive merc shook his head and climbed into the Jeep. ''I'll wait for the rest stop facility at the next tourist information center.''

The travelers set off, already sweating from the growing heat. By midmorning it was so muggy that breathing was difficult. Their clothing became damp and remained that way, hanging like lead on their muscular frames. Beck and Hayes rode in the back seat, stripping, oiling and reassembling the M-16s that

Jessup's Peruvian diplomat had brought from the States.

At noon, less than a hundred miles out of Isipo, they ran into their first roadblock.

The road curved around a stony outcrop covered with thick vegetation. On the other side, a dozen dark green army vehicles, trucks and jeeps, lined the road. Zairian soldiers stood with their weapons ready, fierce and ill at ease, their fingers clasped carelessly around the hairpin triggers of the old Belgian-made automatic FN FAL rifles.

They closed around the Jeep as the driver slowed to a stop, several of them shouting questions simultaneously. Dr. Nzila handed his papers to a sergeant. The bright red official seal was enough. They spoke briefly in Swahili.

"There's been an uprising in the eastern provinces," Hayes whispered to Beck in translation. "The government has mobilized the army in the region and declared martial law."

The sergeant gave Nzila back his papers and waved his soldiers out of the way. As the Jeep pushed forward, Nzila turned to the mercs to explain. His dark brow was furrowed in worry.

"A rebellion. He doesn't know the details, but apparently it was like a flash fire—very sudden. The situation in Isipo is under control with government soldiers occupying the town, but there are still problems near the frontier. No one seems to know how or why it happened even. At least these soldiers haven't been told."

"Soldiers are the last to know," Hayes commented wryly. When they had passed the roadblock, he withdrew the M-16 from its hiding place under the seat and held it, scanning the jungles for the unexpected as they passed.

A few miles later they passed the first refugees, a family led by a man with several wives and half a dozen little children, carrying bundles of possessions on their heads and backs. Soon there were more: trucks filled with old people and the sick, carts pulled by hand carrying women with newborn babies. The trickle became a flood of black humanity, pushed forward by soldiers who shouted and waved their rifles at the slow and the hesitant.

Nzila's papers were given cursory examinations at the next roadblock. An hour later they saw the black smoke curling slowly over the jungle. Isipo was burning.

They passed a final roadblock. This time the sergeant took their papers and radioed his commander. A few moments later he waved them through. Most of Isipo's population had fled. The town was given over to occupation by the Zairian army.

The hospital and some adjacent buildings were smoldering ruins. There had been a slaughter. Bodies punctured by bullet holes dotted the side streets in dark pools of dried blood, swollen like inflatable dolls in the equatorial heat. Grim-faced troops collected the corpses, piling them five deep like cordwood in front of a line of trucks.

Hayes and Nzila disappeared to seek out the officer in charge, leaving Beck and the driver to watch the

horrendous scene. A few moments later they returned, visibly disturbed. A Zairian officer walked
with them, pointing to the still-smoking hospital and
explaining in unhurried English what had happened.

"When the doctors at the hospital did not give to
them the medicine they demanded to protect them
from the Horror, the people stormed the facility,
plundering and looting what medications they found.
They killed many, saying that all with the Horror must
die, but they killed many others, too. Their bodies
were thrown into a hospital courtyard and burned.
The flames spread. Some of the doctors, missionaries
and health workers were also thrown into the fire."

The officer pointed to two soldiers carrying a
charred corpse, thin as a brittle stick, from the street
that ran alongside the hospital.

"We know many were alive because they tried to
flee." He shrugged, unconcerned. "It is like this in all
the villages north and east of here, too. We are not
supposed to know this, but I have spoken to my
brother officers by radio."

"Barrabas, Hatton?" Nate looked at Hayes. The
black man shook his head.

"Two *mzungu* accompanied Dr. Obispo east to
Shibandu three days ago," the officer chimed in help-
fully.

"Lee and Alex," Hayes said to fill in the blanks for
Nate's benefit. "There are some survivors from the
hospital. They remember those two. But no one has
seen a white man with white hair."

"It is impossible for these people to forget such a
man if he existed for them," Nzila added.

"It is the witch doctors," the Zairian army officer went on, apparently not understanding the line of conversation. "They become jealous of the Europeans' medicine. Then the Horror comes."

"And since European medicine is helpless against AIDS," Nzila continued, "they see an opportunity to drive their rivals out."

Hayes looked at the Zairian doctor doubtfully. "I've spent enough time in Africa to know that it takes more than witch doctors to stir people up like this."

Nzila nodded slowly. "I think you are right. But truth and the government's explanation are not always the same. According to many African governments—including the one in Kinshasa—there is no such thing as AIDS here."

"So, what's next?" Beck demanded.

"The colonel here happens to be sending a convoy in half an hour to Shibandu, where your two friends went with Dr. Obispo," Nzila explained.

"A small village, seventy-five miles from here," the Zairian officer explained generously.

"So we go on." Claude Hayes turned for the Jeep, his tone of voice clearly betraying worry.

## 10

Erika Dykstra arrived in Isipo barely half an hour after Hayes and Beck had pulled out. She sighed while the army colonel laboriously explained that they had already gone, and her lower lip trembled with disappointment. She bit down to keep it still. The Zairian officer seemed to enjoy her discomfort. But discomfort was something she was growing used to.

She had made her way out of Kinshasa the day before with little problem, at several points making such good time that she had almost caught up to the Jeep carrying Claude Hayes and Nate Beck. She had slowed, lengthening the gap, and was never noticed in the procession of vehicles, pedestrians and animals that clogged the highway for miles and miles.

Later, the road deteriorated, and she quickly lost time. The taxi had neither the stamina of the Jeep nor an experienced driver. Soon she was forced to creep from pothole to crevice to rut, at a pace somewhat slower than the herds of cattle that she encountered periodically.

Night fell, and almost simultaneously rain, so much of both it seemed that a mean god had dumped buckets full of ink from the sky. The wipers were useless against the torrent, and the headlights not much better at penetrating the dark. When the road crumpled out from underneath the car, pushing Erika almost over her own edge, she pulled over. Even with the windows up, rivers of water dripped through the seams of the windshield and along the tops of the ill-fitting doors. It was impossible to avoid getting wet no matter which way she twisted. The steady drip drip drip on her forehead or shoulder was like Chinese water torture.

When the rain stopped, she opened the window, gasping for fresh air. Clouds of mosquitoes swarmed in, beating against her face and flying into her mouth and nostrils before she was able to roll the window back up. She spat, wiped her tongue on her sleeve and spent the next hour clapping her hands together in the dark in a Sisyphean effort to eradicate the little pests.

The taxi grew hotter, steamier and stuffier with every minute. She decided it was better than being eaten alive by voracious insects and she curled up in the back seat for a long sleepless night.

Morning was a relief.

After filling the gas tank from spare cans in the trunk, she started with the first glimmer of light in the east. She drove with her headlights out and the knowledge that she might be miles behind Hayes and Beck, or stumble across them around a bend in the road. There was, however, no sign of them.

Around noon she began to pass hundreds of government soldiers. They eyed her lazily, mildly surprised at the sight of a white woman driving a yellow taxi from Kinshasa through the jungles of the eastern provinces. No one made an effort to stop her. An hour later she encountered the first roadblock. It appeared disorganized, the soldiers lounging carelessly against the fenders of their trucks, laughing and joking and smoking cigarettes. A few looked up when they saw the taxi approach, but no one made an effort to move. Erika took a deep breath and held her foot steady on the gas pedal.

She smiled and waved out the window as she went by, talking to them loudly in Dutch. Looks of surprise and incomprehension creased their faces. She heard shouts as she passed down the gauntlet of army vehicles, and in the rearview mirror she saw a few soldiers run after her waving their arms. No one shot at her, though. She kept going.

The second roadblock, half an hour later, was more difficult. Her progress was slowed to a crawl by streams of sorry-looking refugees on foot. She pulled to a stop beside a fat sergeant in a ribbon-bespangled uniform, spoke rapidly in Dutch and English and handed him her passport with several hundred zaires.

"Isipo," she said, pointing up the road, adding, "*Je suis avec la Croix Rouge!*"

The sergeant slipped the zaires into the breast pocket of his uniform, handed her the passport and waved her through without a word.

The third roadblock, not far from the smoking town, was different. Here, a senior officer was called. He yelled at her, waving his arms angrily and railing in Bantu. She countered by shouting back at him in Dutch, German, French, English and the smattering of Vietnamese she still recalled from her days in that part of the world. The officer snapped his fingers at some soldiers, and a few minutes later Erika was driving into Isipo under heavily armed escort.

There, the soldiers had lifted her roughly from the taxi and presented her to the surprised colonel who was in charge. Now she learned from him that Nate Beck and Claude Hayes had already arrived and left for the next village.

"What about this man?" she said, fumbling in her shoulder bag for the photograph of Barrabas.

"Ah, the man with the white hair."

"You've seen him!"

The Zairian colonel shook his head. "The others are looking for him, too. No one has seen him." He narrowed his eyes with dawning suspicion. "What is it that interests you and the others about this man?"

Erika thought quickly. "We have business to discuss."

"Business," he said flatly.

"Medical matters."

"Well, you can discuss these business matters with him in Kinshasa, if he is there."

Erika looked at the Zairian colonel, for a moment not understanding. She turned, and got back into the car.

"That's not my intention," she said.

The officer smiled in a slow, relaxed way and leaned on the door. "And what is your intention?" he asked.

"To go on." Erika reached out to turn the ignition but the colonel's hand got there first and snatched the keys away. His voice was now grim.

"*Madame*, you will return to Kinshasa with the next convoy. Until then, you are free to go anywhere in Isipo. But do not try to walk away." An army truck rumbled past, the back piled high with bloody corpses. He taunted her with a smile and bounced the keys in his hand. "You will die in the jungle. And the natives are restless."

THE ROLLING GREEN HILLS that marked the approach to the eastern border of Zaire bobbed up and down above the tops of the jungle trees. Dr. Nzila's driver followed the two army trucks over the sandy trail that led to Shibandu. Claude Hayes sat quietly in the rear seat, studying a topographical map of the province. It was old, and obviously out of date. Shibandu wasn't marked at all, and Isipo was shown to be a small village instead of a town that was a regional center. When he checked the legend, he found it had been prepared for the Belgian government in 1952.

"What's a *mine de cuivre*?" he asked Dr. Nzila, tracing the words in the legend to small shaded marks that appeared periodically up and down the border.

"Copper mine. This region used to be very important for mining copper in the colonial days. Most of the mines were closed after the revolution when the skilled Europeans pulled out. There has been talk of reopening some of them, but I believe it wouldn't be profitable. So the region remains impoverished."

The Jeep bucked over a sudden pothole.

"And the road's bad," Nate added.

They climbed a hill and descended into the lee of a valley, where elephant grass, higher than the roof of the Jeep, grew close to the road on both sides. Sporadically along the plain, squat leafy trees with twisting horizontal branches stood like lonely sentinels. The men rode in silence, the pace of the lead truck unhurried. Twice they stopped for the soldiers to stretch their legs.

"We're almost there," Hayes said, tracing the road on the map with his index finger for Nate's benefit.

The native New Yorker eyed the elephant grass suspiciously.

"I keep thinking we're being spied on," he said. "Every movement in the grass out there. I guess it's just the breezes blowing down from the hills."

"Or someone spying. You may not be imagining things," Hayes said. He shook his head. To himself, rather than to his friend he added a single word of awe in a whisper, "Africa."

The sun was reddish and tipping toward the blue horizon by the time they arrived at Shibandu. They saw the village as they approached by leaning over the sides of the Jeep and craning their heads around the two army trucks. It was little more than a collection of square wattle huts built around several one-story buildings of concrete blocks. One of these was the government health center. The other, off to one side, bore a crudely shaped red cross.

Shibandu appeared strangely silent as the convoy pulled in. Even in the heat of late afternoon, they expected to see children, or mothers pounding manioc root into powder outside each family lodge in preparation for the evening meal. Instead, Shibandu's only inhabitants were well-fed black flies buzzing angrily in the emptiness.

Soldiers piled from the trucks and wandered into the houses, checking for signs of life. They emerged shaking their heads and congregated near the trucks again.

"It ain't good," Hayes remarked, looking in vain for some sign of the vehicle that had carried Nanos and Hatton there.

Nate was silent. A growing sense of foreboding made him restless, nervous. He reached into the Jeep and took out the two M-16s, handing one to Hayes. The soldiers saw the mercs' automatic weapons for the first time. Several pointed toward the SOBs, shouting in Swahili to their officer.

"They don't like seeing anyone but themselves with guns," Hayes told Nate, taking the M-16. It was going to take some fast talking to calm them down.

Dr. Nzila turned to them as several of the soldiers approached. "I will discuss the matter with them. You are my bodyguards."

The stillness was broken momentarily by hidden movement, like a chill draft wafting among the muggy equatorial breezes. There was a rustling whisper so slight that it was barely audible.

Suddenly the air was rent by fanatic high-pitched warbles. The elephant grass along the road parted. Dozens of Africans, stripped almost naked and brandishing machetes, scythes, knives and axes, burst into the open. Their faces were wild, panicked. Someone yelled, exhorting them to attack.

The soldiers ran for cover behind their trucks as torches sailed aloft, descending on the canvas tops. Fed by flammable waterproofing compounds, flames whipped across the vehicles. Soldiers spilled out and backed away from the flames. They opened fire with their ancient Belgian automatics, emptying mags into the first line of attacking villagers.

Soldiers who had been searching the village fled for the cover of the burning trucks. Few made it. Metal, honed to razor's sharpness, flashed. Machetes and axes were raised and fell. Anguished screams broke through the rising tumult. They were cut short.

A second wave, and a third, poured from the cover of the elephant grass, shouting and circling around the trucks to attack the soldiers from the rear. The Zairian soldiers fled singly in all directions and were hacked down by the frenzied villagers.

Hayes and Beck backed against the side of the Jeep forcing Dr. Nzila and their driver behind them for their protection. The driver panicked and ran for the elephant grass just as more men armed with axes jumped out. The axes fell, severing limbs, chopping into head and torso.

"My god!" Nzila muttered, frozen with terror as the two mercs raised their rifles. "It will be a slaughter."

"Them or us," Hayes said automatically. He opened up on the poor driver's attackers as they turned from their bloody work, spattering lead across their chests. Their weapons flew from their hands, and they fell. More men jumped from the grass and ran toward the mercs in a suicidal rush.

Weapon fire from the direction of the army trucks spluttered and died, replaced by frenzied cries and running feet beating against the dry earth. Nate sighted through the open sides of the Jeep. The attackers had finished with the soldiers and turned in the direction of final resistance.

Nate Beck and Claude Hayes stood back to back with the unarmed doctor between them. Waves of savagery closed in on all sides.

ERIKA WANDERED GLUMLY through the little town of Isipo, watching the soldiers watch her while they patrolled the streets and carted away the dead. As she walked she schemed. Since she no longer had charge of the taxi, she needed a jeep. Several were available, with keys in the ignitions. The distraction she needed came to her when she saw a crate of flares amid a pile of metal boxes holding ammunition. She fiddled in her purse until she found the box of cigarettes she had bought in Cairo—it seemed like weeks ago. There were no matches.

Crossing the road to a group of Zairian soldiers, she waved the cigarette, using sign language to ask for a light. One of the guards pointed to the box of cigarettes and to himself with a questioning look. She gave him one. He smiled gratefully and produced a match. He inhaled deeply and looked at the cigarette as he coughed and exhaled a cloud of thick acrid smoke.

"Turkish tobacco," Erika explained.

Other soldiers had moved closer. The colonel was nowhere to be seen. Erika offered them each a cigarette. A moment later they were busy lighting up, inhaling and chattering about the taste of the harsh Turkish tobacco.

Unnoticed, Erika backed away, quickly stooping to take a flare. She turned, hiding it with her body, and walked several yards. She held the glowing ash of her cigarette to the fuse. It spluttered and held.

She turned again, and holding the flare behind her, walked back toward the soldiers, dropping the burning flare into the box it had come from. Maintaining an unhurried pace, she passed behind the soldiers and stood near the jeep.

With a loud hiss, like that of a punctured tire, the flare went off. Brilliant red light glowed from the crate like a radioactive apple, and suddenly gray smoke bubbled up and poured over the side. The soldiers turned, momentarily mystified. One shouted and pointed to the flare. Several of the others shouted louder and pointed at the nearby boxes of ammunition. When the full realization hit them, the rest of the flares went off like a box of Roman candles.

Erika waited a moment as the soldiers dodged the soaring missiles and ran to drag the ammunition crates away. Some decided it was too late for bravery and dived for cover. Erika jumped into the jeep.

By the time she spun it around and headed for the trail that led to the east, her exit was completely obscured by smoke from the flares. She gave herself fifteen minutes before they noticed she was gone. If she was lucky, they wouldn't bother to come after her. Erika Dykstra felt lucky.

She made excellent time on the trail that passed through the hot dry land toward Zaire's eastern frontier. The jeep had the endurance that the taxi had lacked, and she pushed it hard. She found a pair of field glasses attached to the dash. Periodically, on the crests of the rolling hills, she stopped to survey the horizon for clouds of dust that would mark a moving vehicle.

Two hours out of Isipo, she saw her quarry, quite clearly. A Jeep carried four passengers up a hill perhaps a mile away. Behind her, the air was clear. The shadows were growing long with the sinking sun. She doubted she would be pursued with darkness approaching. Then she would have Hayes and Beck— and, she hoped, Barrabas—to herself.

By the time she reached the crest where she had seen the mercs, they had disappeared. She had caught a brief glimpse of wattle roofs not far ahead at the height of the rise, but the road curved out of sight. She had her speech to them memorized, and in her mind she had prepared her words for Barrabas. It was only a matter of getting him alone for a few minutes.

But Erika had a feeling she would have to travel farther to find the man who knew why Gunter lay comatose in a Cairene hospital bed. If he wasn't in Shibandu, the mercs would certainly lead her directly to him.

It was with a chill, then, that she heard the sounds of automatic weapon fire a few minutes later, bursting loud over a chorus of shrill screams. Black smoke rose over the elephant grass. She could only guess, and what she guessed was ambush. She couldn't let it happen. Not now when she was almost there.

She stepped on the accelerator, and the jeep roared, bouncing high over the rough trail, the jolts tearing her arms from their sockets as she clenched the bucking steering wheel. She careered around a bend. The elephant grass opened, giving way to the village houses grouped around the central kraal. She drove abruptly into the midst of the mad carnage, the burning trucks, the mercs huddled behind their Jeep, and the Zairian villagers rushing them, their murderous weapons of wood and steel borne aloft, already bloodied.

Why don't they get into their Jeep and drive away! she thought, cringing in her seat. She hit the horn with the flat of her hand and kept it there, steering her vehicle straight toward the shrinking space between the attackers and mercs. Everyone looked. Axes and spears arced through the air, falling wide of her jeep as she drove in front of the mercs.

Gripping Dr. Nzila between them, Claude Hayes and Nate Beck jumped, landing helter-skelter in a pile of arms and legs in the rear seat. The attackers threw their weapons, heavy steel ax heads and scythes chunking against the sturdy bumpers. Erika flashed a look into the rearview mirror. The main body of killers was venting their rage on the abandoned vehicle. The few in hot pursuit quickly gave up, waving their arms, their curses dying in the wind of speed.

Claude Hayes climbed into the front seat and stared sideways at her, speechless. Nate Beck straightened himself in the back and leaned forward to shout in her ear. He stopped, looked at Hayes, shook his head and slumped back down.

They stopped a mile out of Shibandu.

"You better tell me where I am, guys. All I'm doing is driving."

Hayes was still looking at her in amazement. "I wanna ask you, but I don't know where to start," he said.

"I'm looking for Nile. I know he's here. He left Cairo for Kinshasa a week ago. We have business together."

Hayes shook his head and looked at her earnestly. "Well, Erika, you got the same set of problems and the same set of questions we got right now, and especially the big one."

"What's that?"

"Where in hell's Barrabas?"

**11**

In his first moments in the desert, Barrabas slowly became aware of warmth in his hands and feet. It crept slowly up his limbs, and his fingers began to burn in the hot sun. He could twitch them a little. He tried wiggling his toes and found they moved slightly. In the circumstances, it was the best thing that had happened to him all day. Sensation was returning to his extremities.

There was no respite from heat or sun. It beat through closed eyelids, bathing his vision in neon red. The unprotected skin of his face, arms and hands burned. The dehydration cycle had begun.

His body perspired rapidly, wetting his clothing. The precious body water evaporated, beaten into molecules and dispersed instantly into moistureless air. Sweat dribbled down his forehead and cheeks, pushed by the hot desert winds that brushed him. It stung his eyes bitterly and tickled his skin.

Tiny sand flies found him. Their high-pitched buzzing whined intolerably in his ears as they rejoiced at the banquet before them, trapped and immobile as a pithed frog. They began to sting, sharp bites piercing the flesh of his face and arms. It's good, he thought. The numbness was fading.

He fought to focus his concentration away from the heat, the itching and bites, forcing himself to become aware of every muscle in his legs and arms. He sent orders into his limbs, commanding them to pay attention. His fingers and toes moved, then his wrists and the ankle of his left leg.

The right leg began to hurt, a little at first, the pain flaring quickly to a sharp, steady ache. In the crisis of the moment, he'd forgotten about the bullet he'd taken at the Heliopolis Aerodrome in a gunfight—when was it? Light-years ago. In another galaxy. As the anesthetic of the temporary paralysis wore off, he became vulnerable to a host of new pains that the cruel desert held in store.

Eventually he found he could move his arms and legs, but the muscles of his torso remained unresponsive, and he was unable even to lift his head. He lay now like a thick-shelled bug flipped onto its back, thrashing its appendages in an effort to right itself and save its life.

Slowly, moving from forearm to upper arm, thigh to calf, he flipped his left arm and leg over their partners to the right. The fingers of both hands scratched at the hard desert floor for something, anything to grip. He found it, a crevice in the baked earth, as rigid as set cement. His left foot struck a hard object and wedged against it. He summoned his remaining strength, pulled hard with his arm and pushed with his leg.

He rolled over, flopping onto his stomach. An icy pain flashed through his damaged upper vertebrae. Sharp grit scoured the tender sunburned skin of his face. He brought his arms up, not aware until he lifted his head that the muscles of his neck had begun to respond.

Opening his eyes, he saw for the first time the hell into which he had fallen.

Africa, dry and naked, stretched without limit, cracked and broken by crevices, strewn with rock and clumps of broken boulders. In parts even the baked sand had been scoured away, exposing sheets of hard white bedrock. Heat waves radiated thickly from the earth. It seemed that a chain of mountains lined the far horizon, but the peaks swam in and out of his vision, obscured by a burning white haze undulating along the desert floor.

Turning his head slightly to the right, he saw his parachute. The wind had caught and swept it several hundred feet along the stony desert, where it had snagged on something. Now there were two priorities. The first was to get out of the blazing sun until he recuperated from the injuries of his descent. The second was to find water.

The only shelter available was under the folds of white parachute cloth that rippled in the constant wind. Slowly, painfully, he dragged himself forward, digging his elbows and knees into the cement-hard ground. He crawled on his belly like a worm baking in the sun.

Ages later he came to the rippling white cloth. He pulled himself underneath it, feeling with blessed relief the protection it afforded his bare skin. Needle-sharp pain stabbed up and down his spinal cord with each movement, another good sign, he told himself. In a day, he thought, he would be able to walk.

Looking out from under the parachute cloth, he saw for the first time a sign of life—of what passed for life here. Some brown and brittle branches of dead shrubbery poked from a bank of sand some distance away. Where once there had been life, there had also, once, been water.

Peering carefully at the heat-shifted shades of light and dark, the desert appeared to have been split. It was a wadi, one of the dry, empty gullies that carried water across the desert for a few days during the rainy season each year. The rainy season had ended months ago. Still, there might be water—even if he had to dig for it.

After he had rested for a while, he found he could raise himself slowly on his hands and knees, and with his head up, crawl forward. He bundled the parachute loosely, tied it and slung it over his shoulders. By the time he reached the bank of the wadi, his hands were scraped and raw from the brittle soil.

The wadi was dry.

Rushing streams of water, from rainfalls in the mountains to the west, had carved a ditch into the desert floor with the force of a bulldozer. It slashed straight across the desert, twenty feet wide and ten feet deep. At certain times of the year, shrubbery grew along its banks from seeds that lay dormant under the soil during the dry season. Now, all that was left was a few leafless sticks, their dried root systems barely clinging to the sand. The bottom of the wadi was clay, baked as hard as porcelain in the desert kiln.

He was suddenly more aware of the dryness of his throat; his tongue felt big in his mouth, and his eyes were sticky. Exhaustion overcame thirst.

The yearly rush of water had carved deep ridges under the banks of the wadi, and these were in shadow from the searing sun. Barrabas pulled himself to the edge. The hard, baked grit crumbled under his weight, collapsing in a miniature avalanche down the side of the wadi. Barrabas felt himself dropping and didn't resist.

He rolled down the bank, pain jolting up his back, and came to a stop with his face buried in sand. He forced himself to crawl slowly to the darkness under the bank, where at least an illusion of cool existed. He pushed at the sand, carving a bed to the contours of his body, and lay in it. Pulling the parachute around him, he fell into sleep like a rock pitched into an abyss.

He dreamed towards morning. In silence. Over and over, like a loop of film wound around a projector's reel, Gunter stepped from the airplane, waving. Each time Barrabas felt himself trying to warn Gunter, to save him, but nothing could penetrate the iron silence. It was like having his arms cut off, or his tongue cut out. Each time, Gunter's face exploded in red. The film returned to the beginning, offering him another try, another chance to break the cycle, to do something different, to save Gunter. Each time he failed.

The physical awakening of his body dragged him reluctantly from the dream, and as it faded, Gunter was replaced suddenly by the disembodied face of Karl Heiss, thrown back, mouth open in derisive laughter.

He sat up quickly, drawing his breath and wiping the last burning image aside. First he was aware of his body. The paralysis had vanished, along with the sharp needle-like pain in his back. He was instantly conscious of thirst, the dryness of his mouth, throat and nasal passages. He found some small pebbles and put several in his mouth, moving them with his tongue, collecting saliva to swallow and gain the illusion of refreshment.

For the first time he was able to check his wounded leg. The bullet had passed through the muscle of his calf, leaving a painful, bloody mess and a deep ridge in the flesh. It was caked with dried blood, which had formed a thick protective barrier and begun the healing process. Unless his body received water, however, it would soon become gangrenous.

He tore a strip of cloth from the parachute and bound it tightly. Then he tried to stand. He lowered his weight slowly. It was barely tolerable. Walking would increase the pain. But at least he could walk. The first light of dawn had barely buffed the edge of night. It was cool. He fitted the folds of the parachute over him like a voluminous cape, ripping out swathes to wrap around his arms and legs and tying it to fit his body with the cords. He fashioned a hood, wrapping it around his face until barely a slit showed where his eyes were.

Hobbling slowly up the side of the wadi, he stood at the top without climbing over the edge. In the dawn's early light, the distant rolling crags were silhouetted in darkness against the horizon. He followed them in a circle almost three hundred and sixty degrees around. He appeared to be on a desert plateau, which likely descended on the other side of the mountains. In the Western Desert, civilization was to the east. The wadi carried water in that direction. He limped carefully to the bottom. The baked earth was cracked but as hard as pavement. He started walking.

An hour later the yellow sun floated above the horizon, scorching the tan-brown desert as it climbed higher. The backs of Barrabas's hands were swollen and bright red from second-degree sunburn. He crossed his arms in front of his chest, tucking his hands under his armpits to protect them. The awkward position cost him some of the precarious balance caused by his wounded leg. The increasing hunger and thirst made him light-headed.

He rested ten minutes then walked for twenty, knowing that his survival depended on how well he conserved energy. By midmorning he estimated he had done about five miles. The rays of the sun beat down, roasting the earth. Heat in the clay bottom of the wadi radiated through the thick soles of his boots. There was still no sign of life, other than clouds of mosquitoes that seemed to materialize out of nowhere, sting and vanish as suddenly.

Barrabas decided to retreat from the midday heat into one of the caves strewn under the banks of the wadi. He would continue his trek in the evening when it was cooler. Barely had he begun to climb the bank toward a promising shadow when he heard a noise like rumbling thunder. He looked up at the sky. There were a few white wisps of clouds far away, near the mountains in the west.

The sound came from behind him, muffled by distance, but growing quickly louder. Pebbles danced in the bottom of the wadi, and the ground trembled. He knew what it was and scrambled up the side of the dry riverbed, ignoring the searing pain that shot up his right leg with each step.

A wall of water, reaching almost to the height of the wadi, swept relentlessly down the channel toward him—run off from a freak mountain rainfall. He had prayed for water. Now it threatened to drown him. The edge of the wadi was held together by the root system of a dead shrub. He gripped it, pulling himself up and watching the baked sand crumble away.

The air filled with the deafening roar of onrushing water. Barrabas would be crushed before he drowned. He jumped with his good foot, swinging his legs over the edge of the wadi as the wall of water swept past, and rolled as fast as he could across the sharp stones as the bank crumbled underneath him. When he came to a rest, the roar of the deluge was already fading.

Quickly he staggered back to the edge of the wadi, taking care not to tread too close to the edge. The water was vanishing as quickly as it had come, seeping through the cracks in the clay to the porous sand beneath. Even as he watched, the level in the wadi sank. The tops of boulders that had been washed clean from the banks began to appear above its surface like smooth, bald heads.

Water. All he needed to drink and nothing to carry it in.

Carefully he descended the banks of the wadi again, but his boots were sucked into the wet clay sides and trapped. It took most of his strength to lift each foot from the enveloping sludge, but near the bottom he was able to gain support on the tops of rocks and small boulders. He knelt and pressed his face close to the silted yellow water, scooping up a handful and bringing it to his lips.

The liquid tasted cool and slightly bitter from the sediment, but as it coursed down his throat he had the sensation of a fire going out. He drank and wet his face and drank again. When he felt full, he waited a few moments, then drank more. He drank until the water dissolved into the soil, forming muddy pools that visibly evaporated under the desert sun's simmering heat. In less than an hour, the bed of the wadi was dry, cracking into a moonscape once again.

The water refreshed Barrabas physically, but also gave him the knowledge that he had five more days—the maximum length of time a lucky man might live in this forbidding environment. He began to follow the wadi again, stepping carefully where the soil was still wet, until it suddenly veered to the north. He climbed the bank, searching until he found an overhang that cast a shadow away from the sun. Wrapped in the parachute, he crawled into it and fell into a deep sleep.

When he awoke, the shadow cast by the wadi's bank filled the dry streambed, so that he knew it was already early evening. Hunger growled in his stomach, and his body ached in every joint. Only his thirst had abated. He climbed to the desert floor and looked out across the plateau to the mountains in the distance.

The wadi appeared to continue its course to the north. It was time to go overland.

The wind in the desert was perpetual, blowing fine particles of dust into his eyes and nose. For the first time he was aware of the grit that had found its way through the folds of the parachute and underneath his clothing, now grating against his skin with every movement.

Stars of night appeared, familiar enough to reassure him that he was going due east, and casting a pale luminescence over the flint-strewn desert. The land glinted and sparkled ahead of him, and eventually he arrived at the edge of a vast salt flat, its cracked alkaloid surface stretching as far as he could see. He had no choice but to cross it.

The dried salt crust disintegrated underfoot like thin ice breaking over pools of moist, sucking clay. Each step threatened to trip him. It was a death trap. If he fell, the alkaloids would eat through his clothing and bare skin like lime. The stitching holding his boots together began to dissolve. He had covered more than a mile when burning sensations around the soles of his feet told him that the deadly salts were leaching through the leather. Not far ahead, the land was a dull blackness. The salt flat ended. He rested awhile, watching the stars turn in the heavens, and went on.

Some time later he began to search the broad, flat plain for some sign of shelter to hide from the approaching day. Ahead of him he saw an outline of darkness, some kind of rock formation or promontory rising at odd angles from the desert. As he approached, it took on hard, straight lines, leaning strangely askew.

It wasn't until he was almost on top of it that he recognized the burnt wreckage of the airplane that had brought him from Cairo. It gave him a sick feeling in his stomach that overcame the steady pangs of hunger. How far had he come? he asked himself. Was he going in circles?

As if instinct wanted to answer his questions, he turned around and saw the first full light of dawn rising—in the west.

What hope he had left of survival caught in his drying throat. Two days had been squandered, like the precious water that had seeped into the dry soil of the wadi. The sun rose like a sentence of death across the wasted miles of desert he had just crossed. How could he have made such a mistake? he demanded angrily, cursing the universe for changing the rules half-way through a game he had never volunteered to play. And from somewhere, some knowledge he had gained about desert warfare in twenty years as a professional soldier whispered the answer—false dawn. A phenomenon of the desert.

He turned, and relief showered upon him like a sweet spring rain. The horizon ahead of him had turned white, and the spectral light in the west had begun to fade.

As the sun peeped above the horizon, the first blasts of heat came with it. The desert was again about to become a furnace. Barrabas began to examine the wreckage of the airplane. There was little left except a charred fuselage and a trail of metal debris scattered across the desert. The charred bones of the pilot still lay in the smashed cockpit. There was nothing of use.

He unwrapped the parachute from his body and improvised a low lean to against the side of the wrecked fuselage, carefully calculating where the shadow would fall first. When he closed his eyes, miles of desert slid by, and he dreamed only of walking without rest.

When he awoke he was drenched in sweat, and the pain from his leg was rolling over him in waves. His throat was dry again, bereft of saliva, and his eyelids were like sandpaper. When he thrust the cover of the parachute aside, he realized it was late afternoon. He felt worse than when he had gone to sleep.

A flapping sound captured his attention. Not far away, among the scattered debris that led across the desert to the airplane's final point of impact, the desert winds riffled the pages of a notebook.

Barrabas crawled from his shelter and picked it up. It was the pilot's flight record, dating back several months. Page after page was filled with columns marking latitudes and longitudes, names of African places, and crudely drawn maps. He turned to the last entry. Zaire. Towns named Isipo and Shibandu, and an X carefully placed beside coordinates at a spot near the Burundi border, north of Lake Tanganyika.

He ripped the page angrily from the book and folded it, putting it into his breast pocket. Then he returned to the charred fuselage and wrapped himself again in the tattered folds of the parachute.

On his third day in the desert, his progress slowed considerably. His lips peeled and cracked painfully,

and he limped on a leg that was becoming danger-
ously numb. The wound was infected, and the itchy
sores from the sand fly bites refused to heal. His eyes
dried out, and grit lodged under the lids, so that each
blink felt as if he were wiping them with an emery
board. His tongue swelled in his mouth until it felt like
a dry wool sock. The heat, hunger and thirst made him
dizzy, and his thoughts blurred like a picture out of
focus.

The thin layer of gritty flintlike soil, which barely
covered sheets of sun-scorched rock, eventually gave
way to rolling dunes of sand, rippled into waving lines
by the wind. His feet sank into it, and for each step he
took up the incline of a hill, he slid back half the distance he gained. A sharp movement on one side
caught his eye. He turned just in time to see a tiny
furry rodentlike creature watching him. Food.

He dived for it, but it disappeared, instantly bur-
rowing under the sand. As he moved on, he saw several more of the fast little creatures eying him from a
distance. Each time he made a move for one of them,
they vanished under the desert sand. Crawling on his
hands and knees, he was able to make better progress
on the slithering sandy slopes, and soon he reached the
crest.

The dune plunged steeply down to flat bedrock
again, and in the distance, visible through the thick
wavers of heat, a blue lake sparkled under the high
noon sun. He struggled forward, half falling down the
side of the dune and onto the flat desert floor, in a
headlong rush toward the cool, inviting waters. It took
him only a moment to realize that the lake stayed mo-

tionless on the horizon. There were no palm trees surrounding it, no sign of greenery. Mirage—the juxta-
position of air masses at different temperatures that
made objects on the other side of the horizon appear
closer.

He collapsed, hugging the soil, desperately needing
rest, but knowing that if he didn't go on he would broil
to death under the cruel, hot sun. A big fat blackfly
buzzed his head loudly, and the skin of his left hand
tickled when it landed. Remaining motionless, he
opened his eyes and stared at it, watching it probe a
sore on his skin. Slowly he raised his right hand. He
slapped it, crushing its wings. It fell onto the sand, its
tiny little legs scrambling in the air.

He picked it up and ate it—his first meal in three
days. His mouth salivated slightly, and his stomach
rumbled its thanks for the tiny morsel. Another fly
buzzed his head. He waited again. By the time he was
rested it had been a regular banquet. How many seconds or minutes of life would five flies give him—tomorrow, perhaps even the next day? A few. Every one
of them infinitely valuable.

Barrabas stumbled on, his eyes combing the desert
for shelter, but seeing none. The image of the lake appeared sporadically, sometimes very close, but each
time as he approached it moved away, or disappeared. Occasionally he tried to chase the little
mouselike creatures he had seen earlier. They ran from
him, scrambling along the rocky soil, and with un-
canny intelligence, lost him by running inside the mir-
ages. The dunes returned. He could go on no
farther. His right leg was burning up to the thigh, and

the numbness around the ankle and calf was spreading. With his remaining strength he dug a hole, feeling faint, cool moisture several feet under the surface. This was how the little rodents lived, somehow storing water in their bodies and staying cool in their sand burrows. When the hole was deep enough, he covered himself with the ragged strips of parachute and pulled the sand over him, leaving a funnel of cloth to bring air to his face.

The weight of the sand and the soft contours of his burrow somehow drained pain from his limbs. His sleep was restless, a part of him steadily aware, waiting for the coolness of night to begin and the trek that would lead him on to the morning of the fourth day.

THE NIGHT AIR did little to cool their burning flesh. And although the sun's rays had been replaced by a velvety darkness, their burnt skin cried out for moisture, for relief.

Lee Hatton cringed in pain as she turned her swollen eyes toward Alex Nanos. She only wanted to reassure the Greek, but she couldn't force the words from her parched throat.

She knew it was unlikely that Walker Jessup had understood, or even received her message. And if he had, it was unlikely that Nile and the other team members could make the coordinates in time. Africa was a long way from home.

But Hatton had to believe. For her own sanity and for Alex's sanity, she had to believe that the colonel would come.

The guards laughed at her helplessness, at the look she sent her comrade. They knew her inward strength was meaningless. It would not help her survive the ordeal.

Lee Hatton and Alex Nanos were slowly, but thoroughly, being baked alive.

## 12

In the morning the mirage was still there, appearing suddenly, the image wavering and vanishing, only to reappear on another side, or farther out in the desert. And at times the waves of heat were so thick that they obscured everything beyond a tenth of a mile. Once, when the hot haze vanished for a while, Barrabas saw the mountains he was navigating by, but the peaks and passes had shifted and changed in the night. The sun became his only marker, reducing the world to a single white-hot spotlight that rose from the east toward the center of the sky.

Barrabas stumbled and fell, cutting his hands on the sharp rocks that littered the desert floor. He pushed himself up and on, stumbling a few steps later. Somehow, in this manner, he progressed a distance he couldn't begin to estimate. The searing pain ached from his leg, his tongue was swollen and distended so that he could barely close his mouth, flies feasted on the tiny lacerations festering in his hands, but above all a single imperative screamed, Walk. Or die.

He tripped and fell again, and finally, when his body resisted the command to rise and go on, he knew he was in trouble. The will to live remained; the means did not. There were worse ways to die; the thought swam lazily through his consciousness, uncaring, disappearing finally and leaving his mind empty. The ground trembled and buzzed. He thought it was the blackflies dive-bombing his head, but the noise became louder and more persistent.

It was a motor. His body obeyed, and he stood, staring at another mirage, a wide, shallow lake of cobalt blue surrounded by palm trees. Tiny people in black robes walked near the shore. The image shimmered, as if he were seeing the vision through water. The mirage disappeared in the desert haze, but the drone of an engine grew steadier. It sounded like a small airplane, but where was it?

Barrabas turned, ripping aside the cowl of parachute cloth that covered his head and blinking his eyes against the sticky grit. The desert had come alive.

The undulating waves of heat gave way to the slow procession of a caravan. A hundred camels meandering in single file across the desert flickered in his vision. People in black rode on the backs of the camels or walked beside them. He shouted, or thought he shouted, and waved his arm but they were half a mile off at least and did not respond.

He spun around, searching for the source of the droning noise. The mirage had reappeared much farther away, and the green-spiked tips of palms were clearly visible. Barrabas reached for it, as if he could grab it and pull himself to it, but the vision wavered like a television on the blink and disappeared again into the desert haze.

He noticed for the first time that there were bushes on the desert, scraggly brittle things with a few pale, shriveled leaves. There was a bell tinkling, a plaintive bleating, and suddenly a goat hopped across the desert so quickly that it disappeared almost immediately into the haze.

He pivoted toward the caravan. It was still there, half a mile away and headed in the direction of the mirage. He shouted and stumbled several feet in that direction, but the camels and men plodded on, the line vanishing in and out of the obscuring white haze.

He heard the sound of goats again, and magically, thirty feet away, a row of figures silently regarded him, the hot wind rippling their long black robes. They seemed real, human, but they remained perfectly still. He shouted. Nothing moved except the wind.

The sound of the motor was growing louder behind him, as if an airplane was taking off across the desert. Whatever else might be illusion, the noise was real, and it grew to a deafening roar.

With a shudder Barrabas realized that, hidden in a mirage or by desert haze, he, too, was probably invisible to an observer. An airplane was near, so near it was almost on top of him.

Suddenly, twenty feet away, a small single-engine airplane broke from the white haze. Barrabas yelled and ran toward it, waving both arms frantically over his head. It crossed in front of him, so close that he felt the wash of its slipstream. It lifted from the ground, dipped, rose and soared into the sky, evaporating into the obscurity of distance.

Barrabas stood dizzily, barely able to swallow air through his swollen mouth, unsteady on his feet. He turned slowly in a complete circle, one foot at a time. The caravan was gone, too, vanished into white haze. The mirage of the lake had disappeared. An animal bleated. When he turned to face it, he saw a scrawny white goat eyeing him curiously. He turned one more step. Seven figures gazed at him, unmoving, pillars of stone bound in black cloth and surrounded by brilliant whiteness.

He sank to his knees. The light went out.

LIFE RETURNED gradually, as though a cloud of choking steam were slowly dispersing. He opened his eyes. A beautiful young woman with raven black hair was leaning over him, her face bathed in a golden glow from a nearby oil lamp. Startled, she gasped and jumped back.

He tried to speak but heard little more than a raspy grunt emerge from his swollen mouth.

Immediately she regained her composure and reached for a pitcher. She dipped a piece of cloth into it, wrung it gently and held it to his lips. He gazed at her as she squeezed the cloth. The sweet, cool liquid seeped past his lips and over his tongue. It was water that tasted like honey.

At first he thought it was merely nighttime, but he realized it was cool and windless and that he was inside somewhere, lying on a firm cushion in a small low-ceilinged room. He had mistaken the young woman's headcloth for long black hair, but it was a *tarha*, worn by Bedouin women in the desert and held in place by a chain of gold coins looped around the forehead.

Her complexion was dark, the lines of her eyebrows and lashes finely etched against her smooth, soft skin. Her lips were full and sensuous, ruby red in the soft amber light. She smiled slightly and stroked the side of his head gently. Her fingers were heavy with gold rings, inset with dark polished stones.

He was alive. If he could do nothing but look at this woman's beauty, he was convinced he would heal very fast. Another thought hit him like a hammer. He was dead and this was heaven.

He wanted to touch her, to see if she was still real. She opened her mouth and was about to speak, but another woman entered through a curtained doorway across the room. This one was old and withered, her long black robe gathered over hunched shoulders, her back bent. She uttered an order in a throaty, guttural language. The beautiful woman stood immediately and backed out of his field of vision. Barrabas tried to say something, tried to reach out and take her hand, to hold her beside him, but he was far too weak, and she was gone.

The old woman moved into the room and sat near him. He felt her gnarled hands probe his body, examining the bandages that covered his leg and hands. She took foul-smelling ointment from a small brass dish and smeared it on his skin. She set a small charcoal brazier no bigger than a teacup on a small table near the bed, sprinkled a powder into it and set it on fire. The aromatic smoke was pungent, bitter, and it made him dizzy. She rose to leave as he drifted off to sleep.

When he opened his eyes again, the room was full of men dressed in the long, flowing robes of the Bedouin, their features dark and Semitic. They stared down at him, impassive, unmoving. One of them spoke, and another answered sharply. Barrabas sank again into unconsciousness.

The third time he came to, it was sudden, and he was almost instantly alert. The beautiful woman was kneeling beside his bed again. She carried a brass tray filled with covered dishes.

"Who are you?" Barrabas asked.

"Nara." She set the tray on the low wooden table near his head.

"Where am I?"

Nara shrugged a little. "The desert. Others call it the Sudan. The name of the wadi is Hamiq."

"How long?"

"Two days."

"You speak English."

The beautiful woman nodded. "Eat," she said, gesturing toward the tray. She rose to her feet and disappeared through the curtained door. Barrabas ate.

The tray held generous portions of yogurt, grainy goat's milk cheese, dried apricots, fresh dates and some kind of boiled millet—a king's feast for nomadic tribespeople who often lived on the edge of famine.

Examining his surroundings, he saw that the walls of his room were made of thick woven cloth and that the low ceiling was arched. The floor was covered with colorful carpets. When he bent over the bed and pulled up the corner of one of them, he found the hard, baked floor of the desert again. He was in a tent.

He felt good. Best of all, he was alive. The ordeal in the desert, the four longest days of his life, was over. Although he had pushed on against the heat, the thirst, the hunger, the torments of sand flies and his wounded leg, it had been his instinct to fight back that had saved him, not hope, for he had fully expected to die. Now, only when he was safe, could he admit that and be thankful for the miracle of Wadi Hamiq, and the angel who tended him.

He tested his wounded leg with his hand, exploring the bandage. The hole that had been torn in the muscle had been smeared with the pungent brown ointment he remembered the old woman using. It was tender, stinging as he probed it with his finger. He smiled. The soreness meant the infection was gone. He was healing. It was time to go for Heiss.

He swung his legs out of the bed, looking around for his clothes just as the curtain over the door was thrust aside. The old woman and Nara stared at him. The old one covered her eyes, shouted something and quickly backed out, dropping the curtain closed behind her.

Nara seemed to be smiling. She walked to the low bed and threw a wool blanket around Barrabas.

"A Bedouin woman cares for a sick man as she does for a child, and your nakedness is of no consequence. But now you are healthy and must conceal yourself."

She called to the door in a few words of Arabic, and the old woman entered, casting Barrabas a sulky glance. She hobbled toward the bed, motioning for Barrabas to show her his leg. Once again she began to smear the wound with the foul-smelling brown ointment. Nara cast her eyes down, and dutifully, like a servant, cleared away the tray and dishes.

"I want my clothing," he told her.

Nara turned to the old woman, and they spoke rapidly in the guttural tones of desert Arabic.

"I will bring you clothing," she answered, moving toward the door.

"Who is she?" Barrabas called to her.

The old woman looked up from her ministries to his leg and scowled.

"She is Vashti, wife of Ha'man, who is dead, and mother of Mashiq, leader of this tribe."

"Who are you?"

"I am Nara, the wife of Mashiq. She is my mother-in-law."

MASHIQ BROUGHT BARRABAS clothing. Nara's husband was a young man in his early twenties, handsome, and almost six feet tall. His dark eyes examined Barrabas carefully, glinting with carefully concealed intelligence. He threw an armful of Bedouin robes over the bed.

Barrabas looked at them. "These are not my clothes. I want my own."

"They are burned," Mashiq said. "You will wear these." Unlike Nara's English, his was heavily accented.

Barrabas cursed silently. The navigational map from the airplane that he had put in the breast pocket of his shirt was gone.

"If you're the leader of this tribe, I guess I owe you a great debt for saving my life."

"I have returned you to health, fed you and given you clothing. My duty to Allah is done. Now I have other duties."

Barrabas stood, testing his right leg for strength before putting his weight on it. It was sore enough to be a problem. But not enough to stop him. He reached for the clothing. The long woolen robes were thick, the material rough and scratchy.

"The layers of cloth will keep you cool," Mashiq told him, watching Barrabas inspect the clothing. "This one first." He reached over to touch one that was made of cotton.

"There was an airplane here. When I was in the desert—"

"He has gone to al-Calq and will not return for a month."

"Where is—?"

"One day's journey to the south. By camel."

"And by foot?"

Mashiq stood and moved toward the door. "I have duties to those other than Allah. I must also fulfill obligations to the government in Khartoum if my people are to be left in peace with our old ways of the desert. You have the freedom of the oasis. But you will go nowhere else."

Barrabas stopped dressing and looked sharply at the young Bedouin chieftain. The Sudanese government was a puppet regime of Libya, their northern neighbor.

Mashiq continued. "I have sent word to Khartoum. In two days soldiers will come for you." He strode to the door and pulled back the curtain.

"Where did you learn English?" Barrabas demanded. Mashiq stopped.

"From my wife." He disappeared through the door, leaving Barrabas alone.

WADI HAMIQ WAS LITTLE MORE than a narrow pond of water perhaps a quarter of a mile long. The low black tents of the Bedouin were scattered among the date palms that ringed the water. Barely a few steps beyond the encampment, the desert began again, waves of heat dancing across its blistered sands. The harsh white sunlight beating against his face made Barrabas faintly nauseated for a moment when he left the tent. He pushed against it and found himself squinting at a landscape of sand almost as white as snow. His eyes adjusted after a few seconds.

In the noonday heat, the oasis had the syrupy languor of a slow-motion film. Bedouins went about their daily chores, their long black robes highlighted brilliantly against the whiteness of sun and sand. Men and boys herded docile camels around the end of the pond, while women balanced baskets of laundry on their heads and made their way to the water. Children scurried back and forth among their elders, playing like children everywhere in the world.

Barrabas walked slowly, working through the soreness he felt in his muscles and limping on his bad leg.

Mashiq had been right. The heavy layers of clothing kept him cool, and the *kafireh* wrapped around his head shielded him from the dizzying rays of the sun.

No one paid him any attention except the children, who hung back near the palm trees, staring silently with wide-eyed curiosity. When he looked at them, they laughed self-consciously and shied away.

The cool-looking waters of the oasis drew him, a miracle set in the midst of the forbidding desert. Some teenage children throwing dates from a palm scurried down the trunk and ran as he approached. He stood for a while by the shore of the pond, a pariah, picking ripe dates from the sand and throwing them against the dark glassy surface of the water.

At the far end women washed laundry by hand in the shallow water. One of them left the group and wandered along the side of the oasis in his direction. It was Nara.

She approached him bashfully, casting quick glances around to see that no one was near.

"You have healed quickly."

Barrabas smiled. "With someone as beautiful as you for a nurse, how could I not get better."

Nara laughed, looking shyly away. There was something distinctive about this Bedouin woman. She moved differently than the other Bedouin women. It was as if she held something back, a part of herself, an inner toughness concealed by a docile exterior.

"So now you want to go somewhere in a hurry, and you are planning how to escape from here." Mashiq's wife watched him, and he was unable to tell if the look in her eyes was defiance or teasing.

"What makes you say that?" he asked sharply.

"It must be so. For you to have healed so fast."

Barrabas furrowed his brow, puzzled by her words.

"Among our people," she went on, "we believe that illness or injury happens to a person for a reason, never by chance. When we find a man in the desert, we think this is someone who is punishing himself for something he feels inside. Or is being punished. It is the same for recovery. Whatever has been troubling you has been put aside. Now you have a purpose to attend to. Your body shows it by getting better. Such a recovery indicates you are favored. You have gained allies here."

Nara gave a little shrug. "Of course, you don't have to believe any of this."

"But you do," Barrabas said.

The woman turned away, uncomfortable. She pondered something before replying. "Some of it."

"But you're not Bedouin. What—who are you? Why are you Mashiq's wife?"

"You are wrong. I am Bedouin. I—"

"Where did you learn English?"

She spoke with difficulty, as if it pained her to speak of a life that had taken place in a world centuries beyond the primitive oasis settlement.

"My father took his family from this tribe to work on the oil wells in Egypt, and then into the city. He became very wealthy. I went to school with foreigners. Then he died. My mother soon after."

She paused. Barrabas motioned along the shore of the oasis inviting her to walk. She nodded.

As they moved toward the palm trees, she sighed. "When I was very young—I don't even remember, to be honest—I was betrothed to my cousin Mashiq, in accordance with Bedouin custom. When I no longer had my own family, I was claimed by Ha'-man, Mashiq's father. And when I was nineteen, I was married to him. That was six years ago."

Barrabas fumbled for something to say. He sensed in her words an enormous sadness. Now he thought he saw what caused it—she had been trapped in a world she hadn't made.

"I'm sorry. I guess there was nothing you could do."

Nara stopped and looked at Barrabas with an expression of surprise, then laughed. "No, no. You don't understand. The marriage was not a problem."

"You mean you wanted to?"

Nara nodded happily. "For young people with an arranged marriage, we were lucky. We fell in love. So I stayed with my people and went back to the old ways."

She looked at him, still concealing something. "And you. What about Erika?"

The name of Barrabas's former friend stopped him. "How—"

"When you were lying in bed after we found you, you said many things. That you had to find someone. The name of this woman. Your lover?"

"Used to be. Not anymore. And, yes, I am looking for someone. It's a long story."

She motioned to a shady patch under a cluster of palms.

"So tell me." They sat for a while on the sand, feeling the warm breezes blow in off the desert, and Barrabas told her. She listened carefully, nodding slowly without interruption.

"I want to get to al-Calq," he concluded, angrily tossing a stone into the water and watching the ripples spread across the still surface. "Perhaps I can get this guy with the plane to take me...I dunno. I had a map, but—"

"Is this what you had?" Nara reached inside her robe and pulled out a folded square of white paper.

He took it from her, scarcely concealing his excitement as he gently pried apart the stiff, salt-encrusted paper. When he looked back at Nara, his face was glowing, and she watched him with a grin.

They sat silently for a moment, with Nara gazing over the lake. Barrabas sensed she was preoccupied, and deeply troubled. He was about to ask her when a sharp voice hurled Arabic words at them. They turned to see Mashiq's old mother glaring from thirty feet away. She shouted again and motioned for Nara to come to her. Her withered ancient face was a mask of hostility.

Nara began to rise from the sand when Barrabas put out his hand to stop her.

"Why do you go the moment she orders you? She treats you like a servant. You're the wife of her son who is the tribal leader."

Nara hurriedly pushed his hand away. "You don't understand," she said, standing and brushing sand from her robe. "They are the old ways. I am her servant. A bride must join the family of her husband, and there she must do as the mother tells her.''

"Until she dies?'' Barrabas asked, incredulous. He rose slowly, pulling himself up against the trunk of the palm to ease the weight on his sore leg.

"Until I bear sons.''

Barrabas and Nara looked at each other for an intense moment, and the source of her unhappiness slowly dawned on him. She read in his eyes that now he understood.

"It has been six years, and still we have no children. We love each other, but I cannot make him happy without giving him sons. He will not take another wife because he knows I would live forever as a servant in his own tent. His mother hates me for it and wants me to go. She thinks I am cursed by the evil eye. It is very difficult for Mashiq, as leader of the tribe, to not have sons. So it is because I love him that I want him to cast me away. He refuses.''

From her vantage point thirty feet away, the old woman snapped at them again, waving her arm angrily for Nara.

The beautiful Bedouin woman started to go but turned at the last minute, grabbing Barrabas's arm and pinching the cloth.

"If you are called to a meeting of the elders tonight, you need only be truthful. Remember, you have made friends here. Even Mashiq's mother thinks you are blessed because your recovery was so fast.''

Nara quickly crossed the sand toward her angry mother in-law. Baffled by her sudden advice, Barrabas followed with his eyes as she circled the pond, walking several steps behind the old woman. He saw now what set her apart from the other women at the oasis. She was modern, caught by culture and love in a strange time warp.

And Barrabas felt something else stirring, a fire ignited mysteriously deep inside. There was a word for it.

It was desire.

## 13

At night the sand continued to glow, casting a kind of perpetual evening light. Near objects—the long black tents, the tall palms and the camels shuffling contentedly near the water—seemed clearly defined from their backgrounds while darkness thickened somewhere over the desert. Stars glittered overhead like diamond points in a blue-black sky.

At dinner a boy brought a tray of yogurt, millet and brothy stew to Barrabas's tent. When he spoke to him, the Bedouin youth shrugged, not understanding. Barrabas ate alone, listening as night stole over the oasis, and the camp became quiet.

Yellow oil lamps glowed from some of the larger tents. Barrabas heard the last fading sounds of children called in by their mothers, and finally the voices of men laughing, discussing. The rich aroma of black coffee drifted on the desert breezes. The boy who had brought him dinner reappeared from the shadows of darkness, beckoning.

"You come. To council," he said, his tongue working laboriously over unfamiliar syllables. It sounded like Nara was giving English lessons.

Barrabas followed him among the tents toward the largest one, which he knew to be Mashiq's. A few times, women reached out of doors to pull the flaps down and tie them shut against the night.

Each of the long tents had entrances at both ends. From the side that faced away from the dusty desert winds golden light came, glowing over richly woven carpets, cushions and brass coffee urns. This was the men's side.

The sounds of heated conversation grew louder as they approached the largest, Mashiq's tent. The Bedouin men who were gathered there fell silent when Barrabas rounded the corner and stood before them.

Mashiq's quarters were more lavish than any of the others. A small fortune in elaborately woven carpets hung on the walls and floor. A dozen men, varying in age, squatted on silk cushions. Beside each, small carved tables of inlaid wood held gold cups steaming with thick black coffee. Near Mashiq, a large brass coffee urn sat over a raised iron hearth, heated by glowing coals. A teenage boy ground coffee beans by hand in a china mortar. The other young men of the tribe had also been allowed, and took up positions along the walls behind their elders.

For a moment no one moved. Barrabas was silent and stern, watching the Bedouins watch him, casting his eyes against theirs one by one. Mashiq stood.

"Allah has brought you from the desert, and it is my duty to give you hospitality. As my guest, I must also protect you. I bid you welcome."

The Bedouins arose simultaneously in response to the age-old ritual, bowing slightly, but it was obvious that the welcome was lukewarm in some quarters. As they sat again, several of them leaned to each other, muttering softly and eyeing the stranger darkly.

Mashiq motioned to an empty cushion, strategically placed next to the wall of the tent. Barrabas carefully removed the sandals before crossing the carpet. Several of the men looked at one another, nodding in approval.

One of the young men brought Barrabas a small gold cup of coffee. They waited without speaking for him to accept it and sip the hot, bitter liquid. He did it slowly, glancing about the tent and studying his surroundings. The Bedouins were well armed. The wooden stocks of what looked to be AK-47 assault rifles poked from behind the cushions. And there was a heaviness under their robes that suggested mag belts.

When he had sipped, there was an audible sigh. The Bedouins turned their heads expectantly from Barrabas to Mashiq. The young leader continued.

"Unfortunately, there are times when my duty to Allah and my duty to the government in Khartoum conflict. There are very strict orders that American spies found in the desert are to be turned over to the soldiers."

"I'm not a spy," Barrabas said flatly.

Mashiq nodded. "I understand. But convincing the soldiers will be difficult. You will likely be executed after you are tortured, whether you confess or not." He turned to the assembled elders and translated. The heads of several of the patriarchs shook with agreeable enthusiasm. Others looked more distant. Now the purpose of the meeting was clear to Barrabas—he was already on trial. And his life was in the balance.

"I have already heard that you have a story," Mashiq continued, looking directly at Barrabas. "We are ready to listen to it, to see if you can convince us why we should not fulfill our duty to Khartoum."

Remember, you have allies, Barrabas thought, recalling Nara's hurried advice. Had Mashiq decided to be one of them? Why? On Nara's urging? And why would the strange Bedouin woman trapped between two worlds care? He was convinced that there was a hidden agenda at work, and that somehow he was only a pawn in a larger scheme. Whatever it was—and for whomever's benefit—at least he was being offered a chance to talk his way out.

Slowly Barrabas started, carefully trying to outline salient details, but as he spoke his anger churned and the words became passionate. He told the story of persistent evil in his life, a man named Heiss who came back from the dead, each time trying to touch him, to destroy him. He told how Heiss traded the lives of young soldiers for drug profits in Vietnam, betraying his nation.

When Mashiq translated, a chorus of angry murmurs circulated among the gathered Bedouins, and some nodded angrily. Barrabas knew he had struck a chord, and pressed on. He told how Heiss had taken a beautiful woman as bait to lure Barrabas to his death.

The nodding approval of many of the elders gave Barrabas hope that he was succeeding. Abruptly an older man stood, facing Mashiq, but speaking to the others.

"We have fulfilled our obligations to Allah by giving him water and food," the old man whined. "Now we must give him to the soldiers, for that is also our duty."

The older man's son stepped forward. "If we do not give him up, the government will interfere with our lives. Our women and children will be taken to towns and resettled. Our way of life will be destroyed."

A third man rose to speak. "Our caravans will be stopped and searched. They will say we are selling guns, like Atbar."

Barrabas picked the name from the incomprehensible flow of Arabic, suddenly jarring something in his memory, and he fought to remember. The image of the Nubian in the garbage dumps of Cairo flashed into his mind. Al-Hakim had told him. He turned to Mashiq.

"Atbar, a Nubian. He leads caravans of contraband through the Sudanese desert."

The Bedouin leader's eyes glinted when Barrabas mentioned the name. He raised his arm to stop the outpourings of debate and spoke loudly over the others, his voice clear and commanding. "Wait! The stranger knows of Atbar!" The protests ebbed, and the opposition reluctantly returned to their seats. Mashiq signaled to Barrabas. "You know this man?"

"I met him once," Barrabas said slowly, resisting a smile. "In Cairo. He's dead."

A gasp rose from the gathering when Mashiq translated.

"You killed him?" the astonished leader asked.

Barrabas shook his head. "He was sent to kill me. One of the Zabalin saw him attack and killed him with a knife. He was sent by the man I am searching for." He finished his story, telling them how he had come to be in the desert. They listened calmly, some with interest, others with suspicion, and when he finished they turned to Mashiq.

"Atbar is an enemy," the Bedouin leader explained. "He smuggles weapons and slaves, but it is our caravans that the soldiers choose to harass. And when Atbar's pickings were slim, he raided the tents of the *asilin*, the Bedouin nation."

But the older man at the far end of the tent stood, raising his clenched fist angrily in Barrabas's direction.

"This story is a lie. What else would an American spy tell us? And even if it is not, we cannot take responsibility for him. It is pointless to listen further. Let the soldiers decide if he is an honest man, not us."

The young men gathered near him broke out in shouts, echoing his words. Mashiq stepped forward with his hands up, urging silence.

The angry shouts rose higher. The young men gathered by the old patriarch cried contemptuously, "To the soldiers! We must protect our people."

Mashiq strode to the center of the circle of elders, leveling his arm in the direction of the older patriarch, his eyes brimming with fury.

"Habram, you will silence your sons. I am the chief of the tribe. I will take the advice and counsel of all the elders, but not insults! The final decision is mine."

"The tribe has many sons," Habram said pointedly, "who can decide."

The patriarch and the young men sat in cold, stony silence. The other Bedouins turned their eyes awkwardly away from Mashiq.

Finally another Bedouin stood, one who had remained silent and impassive during the heated debate. He faced Mashiq.

"We have heard from the stranger, and from those who would turn him over to the soldiers. Our duty to the government in Khartoum is clear, as Habram and his sons have forcefully told us. But we also have a duty to the Bedouin nation, and to our honor."

Another man rose and addressed the elders. "The stranger has brought us word of the death of Atbar, and it is our tradition to reward the bearers of good news. If they find the stranger gone when they arrive, they will be angry, unless they are given a reason for his disappearance. They think us a stupid people, so perhaps it need not be much, but without that, he must go to the soldiers. The duty of our leader is to his own people first, not to the stranger, and not to Khartoum. I leave it to Mashiq to decide."

Rumblings of discontent rose again from the men gathered near Habram, then suddenly there was movement at the opening of the tent. Nara stood before them, the desert wind rippling her long black Bedouin garment. The soft amber light of the oil lamps burnished the gold chains around her neck and headcloth.

Mashiq looked at her, unable to conceal his shock.

"What are you doing?" he cried, aghast. "It is not allowed for woman to be present at the council of the elders!" Habram's sons elbowed each other, scarcely able to control their smirks.

Nara spoke to him, her voice ringing through the tent with dignity.

"There is a way. It is the way of the *mu'tah*."

"She is right!" a Bedouin broke in, speaking directly to Mashiq. "That will free us from our obligation, for the stranger will no longer be an American, but a Bedouin of the tribe!"

"But to whom?" another said. "Who has a daughter to spare, and who shall we send from the tribe."

Nara stepped forward into the tent, addressing the gathered elders.    "I will go from the tribe," she told them. She turned her fierce dark eyes toward her husband. "You must let me go."

"No!" Mashiq cried, his voice reflecting the torment that showed in his face. He stepped toward Nara. "I cannot—"

"You must!" Another voice, aged and compelling, burst through the opening in the tent. Vashti entered, hobbling slowly into the light to stand beside Nara. She pointed to Barrabas.

"Allah condemned him to trial in the desert for his own reasons. The stranger was tested and survived. He is blessed, a lamb of Allah. His fate is also ours because he has been sent to us."

Vashti turned to her son, her voice softening. "Nara must go, Mashiq. This man must escape the soldiers. Through the *mu'tah* he can do that. In exchange, he must promise to return with her to Cairo, when the *mu'tah* will be ended.''

"Let me go. End our marriage.'' Nara repeated, gazing steadily at her husband.

For a moment Mashiq's face seemed to collapse under the weight of enormous pain. He steeled himself, aware of the eyes trained on him, of the leaders of the tribe who waited for his decision.

"The council is ended,'' he said, looking at Nara, not at the men. "I shall inform the tribe of my decision before morning.''

With those last words, he pulled aside the cloth that led to the inner rooms of the tent and disappeared.

The assembly drifted apart. Barrabas had understood nothing except that Mashiq faced opposition in his own tribe, and that his fate as leader hung in the balance. Barrabas's fate had yet to be decided.

The Bedouin youth who had attended him earlier appeared and accompanied him wordlessly back to his tent. There, he lay on the cot, torn between a desire to sleep and the thoughts that buzzed through his head. Sometimes he tried to make sense of what was happening. Sometimes he thought of Nara.

It was just after midnight when the youth reappeared, motioning for Barrabas to follow. Again he led him across the silent encampment into Mashiq's tent. The Bedouin leader stood near the brass coffee urn, his face a mask of misery. Nara and her mother-in-law sat silently on silk cushions. Neither looked up as Barrabas entered. Another man who had been at the council was also present.

Mashiq motioned for Barrabas to sit. He began to speak, slowly searching for the words, his voice weighted with an overwhelming sadness.

"There is only one way for you to escape the soldiers. That is the way of the *mu'tah*. The *mu'tah* is a temporary marriage, when a soldier makes an agreement with a woman to last for a specified term—a day, a month perhaps, or the length of a war or a caravan. We are willing to make an agreement with you."

Mashiq explained the plan. He would divorce Nara. Barrabas and Nara would enter into a term marriage. They would be given a camel and leave the village immediately for al-Calq. Barrabas had to agree to take Nara to Cairo. When they arrived there, the marriage would be automatically dissolved.

"We will tell the soldiers of the *mu'tah* and brag about the bride price that you paid. They will think we are just greedy fools, selling off our daughters for gold. They will be angry, but they will leave us alone. And you will be safe. Do you agree?"

Barrabas looked at Nara. The beautiful Bedouin woman met his gaze calmly, her eyes filled with the distant peace that came when a difficult decision had been made.

He turned to Mashiq. "I agree. On one condition. You also give me a weapon for the journey."

"You will be cared for," Mashiq said.

Nara stood and crossed the room to her husband.

"Now," she said. "The witnesses are present."

Mashiq put out his arms, placing his hands on Nara's shoulders.

"I divorce you," he said bravely. There was a long, heavy silence, cut by the ragged sounds of Vashti's heavy breathing.

"I divorce you." This time Mashiq's words came slowly, with difficulty. Nara gazed at him steadfastly, waiting for him to complete it by repeating the sentence a third and final time. Mashiq's mouth fought against the words until finally they came, torn from his heart.

"I divorce you." His arms dropped, and his shoulders slumped heavily. The Islamic divorce was complete. A tiny smile flickered on Vashti's face. Without further word, Mashiq strode from the tent, his face trembling with emotion. Nara turned to Barrabas.

"Come," she said, extending a hand. "To be my husband."

They stood together before the old man with the beard as he recited practiced words over a thick leather-bound book. A few moments later he stepped back. It was done.

Vashti stepped forward, carrying a heavy casket the size of a shoe box. She set it on a low table and turned back the lid. It was filled with gold jewelry. Quickly she lifted the pieces out, placing bracelets and necklaces around Nara's wrists and neck.

"It was my dowry," Nara explained to Barrabas. "I am entitled to have it back if I divorce."

Mashiq appeared at the entrance to the tent and motioned them outside. A camel towered over them, its twin humps outlined in stark relief against the star-filled sky. With unconcerned dignity, it sank on its knees to the sand. A leather saddle between the humps was tied with bundles of supplies and water. Mashiq showed Barrabas how to sit sideways, spreading his long Bedouin robes underneath him as a cushion.

"You will need the cushion after several hours," he said, flashing a quick smile. "And this." He hoisted an AK-47 and tossed it to Barrabas. Then he held out a mag belt. The mercenary took it, catching Mashiq's hand and holding it for a moment.

"I will take her safely to Cairo. I promise."

"She is no longer my wife," the Bedouin leader replied. "Therefore it no longer matters." He pulled his hand away and walked toward the tent. At the last minute he turned.

"I trust you," was all he said.

They rode through the night with barely a word passing between them. The camel was slow but steady, settling into an even lopsided pace that took them far into the desert. The harsh, forbidding environment now seemed pleasant under a black-velvet sky whitened by stars, which gradually melted into the silvery light of a rising gibbous moon.

Barrabas and Nara shared the saddle, she riding in front of him, he holding the single rein. She nestled against him and rode open-eyed through the desert, her mind far away.

They stopped for water after several hours and threw straw down for the camel. It munched contentedly. The silly beast always looked as if it were smiling, pleased simply to be aware of everything going on around it.

Barrabas swallowed a mouthful of water and handed the canteen back to Nara.

"You okay?" he asked, his voice still husky from his ordeal in the desert. She tucked the canteen into a pouch on the side of the camel and turned to face him.

"It's not easy. But I made a decision. Now I will live with it. And Mashiq will have sons who will bring him happiness."

"And you?"

"Who knows. At least we can have happiness apart instead of sadness together."

Wordlessly she reached for the chain of golden coins circling her headcloth, removed them and unwound the cloth. As she pulled it away, long black hair with a sheen as glossy as a raven's wing tumbled down her shoulders. Moonlight shone across her upturned face, outlining her sensuous lips. Her eyes were dark.

"Tonight I shall ride as a woman again, not as a Bedouin."

"Yes." Barrabas pulled on the rein. The camel bent its legs and knelt before them. "It's a long way to Cairo."

Nara gave him a strange look before climbing back on. "Yes. Very long."

They arrived in al-Calq in the morning, just as the heat was beginning to build. The oasis was larger than Wadi Hamiq, with a hundred whitewashed mud houses built under palms at the edge of a small lake. Village life had already awoken, with women doing laundry by the lake while the men and boys tended the farm animals and little gardens beside each house. The Bedouins from an encampment next to the village eyed them curiously, reading the name of their tribe from the style of the camel's saddle and the pattern on their headcloths.

They stopped in the tiny square opposite a little mosque with a single curved dome. Nara made inquiries among the people about the man with the airplane. It was apparent from the curses and looks of distaste on their faces that the pilot was not popular among the villagers. Finally one man pointed, and they followed a street that wound around the lake and turned out of the village on the other side.

The battered Quonset hut was well beyond the last house, where the desert was flat and bare of sand and a gravel strip had been plowed across it. A wind sock bobbed at the top of a pole. The old German camouflage markings were still visible on the corrugated tin sides of the semicircular structure. It was a relic from World War II. Inside, someone was cursing a blue streak. As they approached, Barrabas recognized the familiar sounds of American cussing.

A small man with a head of curly blond hair bent over the engine of a Cessna, wrenches in hand. He turned just as they walked inside, his arm back to throw the wrenches in a fit of anger.

"Goddamn Arabs! Get the hell out of here! And take your goddamn sand with you, too." He let out a string of abuse and hurled the tools in their direction. The wrenches fell wide. The pilot grabbed new tools from the tray beside him and stuck his arms back into the engine.

Barrabas jerked his *kafireh* off.

"Hey, bud. Wanna do business with an American?"

The pilot glanced up from his work. There was unconcealed astonishment in his eyes when he saw Barrabas. He was absorbed again by the engine and spoke without looking up.

"Where'd you stumble in from, man? The fucking desert? Park your carpet and I'll be with you soon's I... Goddamn it, that's it!" His hands broke free of the engine compartment, brandishing screwdrivers. He looked jubilant.

"I got nuttin' against Arabs," he said, wiping his hands on a greasy rag as he walked toward them. "But their goddamn desert gets to me. Ever try to keep an airplane flying when even the air is half full of sand?"

His leathery skin was deeply tanned and furrowed with laugh lines at the corners of his eyes. Humor shone in the icy blue eyes. On his forearm, a tattoo of a bleeding heart with a dagger through it was surrounded by a message faded by the passage of years.

"Holy shit. You did come in from the desert, didn't you?" the pilot exclaimed when he was close enough to see the barely healed sores across Barrabas's lips. "What happened? The Bedouins pick you up or something?" He thrust out a hand. "Jack Sawyer. Malibu Beach born and bred. Haven't seen it in more than a decade."

"Nile Barrabas. And this is Nara. I need you to fly us to Cairo as soon as possible."

Jack Sawyer looked at them, smiled and cracked his chewing gum. "And what you plan on using to pay for it, Mr. Barrabas? American Express? The last guy who wandered into al-Calq and said take me to Cairo was General Rommel. That was forty odd years ago, and he didn't make it either.''

''With these,'' Nara said quickly, stepping in front of Barrabas. She thrust out a handful of bracelets and rings made of solid gold. ''And not to Cairo. To Zaire. Near the Burundi border.'' She turned to face her astonished temporary husband. ''You have the map. You show him.''

''You're crazy, Nara. What has to be done there is for me alone. First, I'll take you to Cairo.''

Nara shook her head stubbornly. ''But you told me how urgent it was. That this woman might be taken by this man. That you have friends in danger there. We must go there first.''

''That's impossible. I promised Mashiq—''

''That you would take me to Cairo, but no one said when!'' Nara was shouting.

Jack Sawyer watched the argument with evident mirth, looking from man to woman and merrily cracking his gum.

''A ride to Cairo,'' Barrabas told him.

''No!'' Nara cried, snatching the handful of jewelry away. ''Not with these. I have used you to escape from the tribe and to leave Mashiq with his people. I cannot allow you to betray your friends because of me.''

Her voice softened, and she approached him, looking into his face, her eyes urging him to agree. ''We will go to Cairo, I promise you. But first you have your duty.''

''She loves you, buddy.'' Jack Sawyer jerked his thumb toward Nara.

"She's my wife," Barrabas protested, before he realized what it sounded like.

"Better and better." The pilot shrugged.

"I want you to take us to Cairo."

"Zaire!" Nara shouted.

Sawyer looked at Barrabas. "Well, what have you got to pay me with, buddy? A check?"

"Nara?"

"No."

Jack Sawyer popped his gum. "Zaire," he said, striding back toward the plane. "Good. I was going in that direction anyway."

## 14

Hayes, Beck and Erika discovered the lair of evil at the copper mine the next morning. After camping for the night several miles east of Shibandu, they awoke early and had Nate climb to the top of the highest tree on the ridge of a foothill to pinpoint their location.

The sky was clear in the early morning. The rain clouds were still in the north, gathered like the folds of a wedding dress around the distant snow-covered peaks of the Virunga Mountains. But closer at hand, half a mile up the road, vultures had gathered on the gaunt branches of a dead tree, their stooped shoulders hunched, their concentration focused on something below.

The mercs found the burnt Land Rover there. The corpses in the front seat had been reduced to skeletons. It stood in a clearing on the road like a signpost to hell, warning them that to go farther meant death.

The mercs and Erika stared in silence for a few moments. There was no way to tell if the charred remains were of those they were searching for.

Claude Hayes suggested they do further reconnaissance on foot, overruling Dr. Nzila's plea that they walk through the jungles around Shibandu to get back to government lines at Isipo. The Zairian waited by the jeep while the other three scaled the hill and looked down over the secret compound.

"Whaddya figure?" Nate asked the others.

Claude Hayes trained the field glasses on the facilities.

"Generators, fuel storage, helicopters, satellite dish. One of the buildings looks like it has a huge refrigeration unit. Everything camouflaged." He handed the binoculars to Nate.

"Guerrilla unit?" Beck asked. "Maybe ANC or Cubans or something."

Hayes shook his head. "No guerrilla unit in Africa is as well financed as this outfit. And if you look closely, there are no markings on the uniforms of any of the guards. No flags. Nothing. It's private, whatever it is."

"It's where Barrabas is," Erika said sharply.

The two mercs looked at her.

"I know it is. Where else could he be?" Beck said.

"Well, I'm not going in knocking until I know a little more about who's down there," Hayes grumbled.

Nate sketched a quick map of the compound, marking carefully the sites of the buildings and the distances involved. They set off down the hillside, making good time until they were only a few hundred yards uphill from the jeep. Hayes put out his arms to stop the other two and pointed.

At the bottom of the hill, barely visible through the tops of the elephant grass, a patrol of black soldiers in dark green uniforms had surrounded the jeep. They were heavily armed. Dr. Nzila stood with his arms high while a big man with leopard-skin epaulets on his shirt stepped down from his camouflage-painted vehicle and examined documents.

"Get out of here!" Erika told them. "Go!"

Nate dived for her, but she was too fast.

She jumped past Hayes and ran down the hillside, waving her arms at the soldiers. Nzila was knocked to the ground, and men spread into the elephant grass. The officer moved carefully behind the cover of the jeep, searching for the source of the shouts.

Nate jumped to his feet, ready to dive after her when Hayes tackled him.

"Hey, man, we can't take responsibility for lunatics, or none of us will get out of here alive," he muttered, rolling in the grass as Nate struggled to push him off. He pulled Nate to his feet behind the cover of some low shrubs.

Erika had stopped several dozen yards from the jeep, with her hands up, watching the soldiers circle her warily. The officer had come forward, scanning the hillside with sharp eyes. None of his men appeared enthusiastic about searching further.

Dr. Nzila saw his chance. He ran for the elephant grass. The officer swung around, drawing his revolver, and fired once. A red hole blossomed in Nzila's back as the doctor dropped. The officer shouted an order at his soldiers and Erika was pushed into his jeep. The soldiers piled into a troop carrier and the patrol disappeared up the road toward the copper mine.

"What in hell did she think she was doing?" Nate exclaimed as the soldiers disappeared.

Hayes shook his head. "I dunno. She had something up her sleeve, though."

"Think they'll come after us?"

"Uh-uh. She told us to get out of here. I dunno what's going on, Nate, but I'm into waiting until tonight for a little look-see."

Beck nodded. "And we got all day to think up a plan."

ERIKA WAS TAKEN BRUSQUELY inside the colonial house at the edge of the open pit and pushed into a cool, darkened room. The lamp on the desk had its shade drawn back so that the light blinded her, concealing the voice that spoke to her.

"Welcome, Erika." The words were cold, clammy. "So it *is* you."

She shivered at the cool air, searching through her peripheral vision for the presence of others. They were alone.

"How long have you suspected?"

"From the beginning. You sent the letter from his lawyer, didn't you?"

"Breaking into Heinzmuller's Zurich files was easy."

"But not necessary. You don't seem to understand. Nile and I are a dead item. History. He went crazy. Now he's killed my brother. And I'm here to kill him. Give him to me, Karl Heiss."

The man behind the desk stepped forward, adjusting the shade of the lamp down so it cast a more even light. Erika almost gasped when she saw him.

The scars that lined the side of his head were livid and shiny and as thick as fingers. His head grew from his shoulders like a bullet. But his eyes were the worst. They were black, like husks of charcoal, burned out and dead. She controlled her shock. Everything depended on her performance now.

He smiled at her and slowly raised his hand. Between his thumb and index finger he dangled the small handgun which the guards had found in her purse.

"And this, I suppose, is for him?"

"That's right." Erika bravely stepped forward, extending her hand for it.

Heiss threw it onto the desk. "You must think I'm a fool, Erika."

"All I want is Barrabas. I'm no friend of his. So there's nothing between you and me anymore."

"Are you saying I am forgiven?" Heiss smiled uncontrollably, enjoying Erika's words.

"I want to kill him. Afterward, I'll leave and you can go on with whatever you're doing."

At this point Heiss laughed, bending his body back instead of his head. He turned from Erika and marched to a sideboard, where he clunked ice into glasses. "Vodka, my dear?" He didn't wait for an answer. He splashed soda on top of the vodka and handed her a glass. "To the imminent success of my current project, Erika. And to your noble sentiment in wanting to rid the world of Nile Barrabas."

He chinked his glass against hers before raising it to his lips.

Erika drank. "And what is your latest project?"

"Same old thing, Erika. Destabilization. My clients stand in the shadows ready to pick up the pieces of Western civilization and reassemble them in their own likeness. They are hard masters to please. But they have the resources to pay for favors. It's amazing, for instance, what brilliant scientists will do for money, fame, glory, the opportunity to break new ground, to win eventually the Nobel Prize. In a sense, that is a cheap price for us to pay. And they have done wonderful things for us."

Heiss walked to the window and pulled aside the wooden shutters. The compound was bathed in the white hot sun of the equatorial afternoon. Heat radiated off the rock walls of the cliffs and crumpled tailings of broken rock. A thick shaft of light fell into the room, outlining motes of dust floating in the conditioned air. Heiss stared at his African kingdom.

"And what have they done for you this time?" Erika asked, remaining where she was on the far side of the study.

"Developed new modes of transmission for the virus that causes AIDS. Cultured vast quantities of it by infecting Africans and collecting their blood. Concentrating the contaminated plasma in order to infiltrate it into blood supplies throughout the Western world. We are just finishing up. Hastening our collection procedures by using force is what set off the rebellion in the eastern provinces. But tonight we will ship everything out. By morning I will be gone, along with everyone else, and this facility will revert to its former status as an abandoned copper mine."

He turned from the window and motioned to her. "Come here, Erika dear. Stand by my side."

Erika braced herself and crossed the room to stand in the outside light. Heiss pointed out the window.

"Perhaps you missed seeing that on your way in."

Erika felt her stomach roll in agony. Lee Hatton and Alex Nanos, their half-naked bodies battered, bruised and swollen, were being strung up by their arms on a rack.

"I put them out in the sun for a few hours every day just to remind them who's boss. Otherwise they haven't been very cooperative. I will have them executed tonight before we go. In fact, Erika, I will have you execute them. To prove yourself to me. And, in exchange, you can come with me. Alive."

Erika shook her head. "It's not them I want. It's Barrabas. Let me prove myself by having me kill him."

Karl Heiss placed his hand on the back of Erika's neck and stroked her softly. His fingers were cold and damp. A creepy flutter rippled through her. "I'm afraid that's not possible, my dear. Barrabas is dead. He died in the desert a week ago. But they are his friends. You may take out your vengeance on them."

Erika shuddered. The long journey was for nothing. Her plan had failed and now she was a prisoner—in the lion's den.

BARRABAS LEFT al-Calq that morning, sharing the cockpit of the Cessna with Jack Sawyer. Nara was content to ride in the fuselage with the mysterious crates Sawyer was delivering to Zimbabwe. The pilot flew east to the Nile, which slithered across the desert like a blue snake amid a thin line of palms and a narrow patchwork of marginal farms.

As they approached the urban sprawl of Khartoum, the sand gave way to dry scrublands, pocked sporadically with signs of human settlement. But the Nile was always busy, with Sudanese farmers hoeing fields by its shores and fishermen working in the white-sailed naggars they had used for centuries.

Gradually the landscape changed to foothills and forest as they flew over the rumpled length of the Sudan. Hundreds of tributaries of the Nile, large and small, branched across the continent, their banks home to crocodiles, hippopotami and thousands of multicolored birds. Great cats could be seen trailing herds of zebra and gazelle.

They stopped at the halfway point of the sixteen-hundred-mile journey to refuel in a town in southern Sudan. Nara sat by herself with a needle and thread. At Barrabas's request, she took the dark outer Bedouin robe he wore and expertly refashioned it into Western-style pants and a waist-length jacket. Sawyer studied the crude navigational map Barrabas had found in the desert, comparing it to charts of his own.

"According to my calculations, I'll be dropping you dead center in the middle of nowhere," he told Barrabas. "Shibandu probably boasts more cows than people. Isipo's the regional center, but there's nothing there."

"But that's not what the coordinates mark," Barrabas pointed out.

Sawyer shook his head. "Nope. The coordinates put you smack dab in the middle of nowhere, at the edge of the mountains on the Burundi-Zaire frontier. There ain't nothing there, man."

"What's this?" Barrabas jabbed his finger at a small mark on the map.

"Abandoned copper mine. The mountains are full of them."

"That's it. That's where I want to go."

"You sure?"

"No. But close enough to get a cigar. What are you carrying in those crates in back of the plane?"

"Few little goodies for the boys in Zimbabwe. If you don't ask me no more questions, I won't have to tell you no more lies."

Barrabas pointed to the faded tattoo on the pilot's grizzled arm. "You get that at Quang Doc?"

For a second Jack Sawyer's composure was ruffled. He looked at Barrabas for a moment, then said "How'd you know?"

"Because I remember, afterward, when all the patrols got back to the base camp with almost seventy per cent casualty rates, there was a guy in one of the platoons did tattoos. A heart with a dagger through it. There was a lineup for two days because the ones who survived never wanted to forget they made it back. What's it say? When I die I know I'll go to heaven because I already spent my time in hell?"

Sawyer swallowed and spoke in a whisper. "You were there, too."

Barrabas stood and walked back to the waiting plane.

When they began the journey again, the foothills steepened, the jungle became thicker, and ahead, snow glinted on the sixteen-thousand-foot-high peaks of the Mountains of the Moon.

A storm front moved north against them as they crossed into the forests of Uganda, dumping showers like waterfalls. The Cessna was too small to fly over the disturbance, and too small to survive the force of the torrential rain if it got caught underneath.

"We got plenty of places to land if we have to," Jack Sawyer assured them over the noise of the engines and the windstream. "But I gotta get these crates to Zimbabwe by tomorrow morning."

All Barrabas could see below was impenetrable jungle. But Sawyer plowed on, unconcerned. He steered the Cessna expertly around the downpours as if he were dodging bump cars at a midway.

By early evening, the long, flat surface of Lake Tanganyika was visible to the south, and below them was the rolling green landscape of Burundi.

Nara pushed herself forward almost into the front seat and pointed to a hillside far below.

"Look there with your binoculars," she told Barrabas.

He saw a tiny waterfall, not much bigger than a bathroom shower, pouring down the face of a rock into a stream. High on top of the rocky hill, there was a small stone pyramid, not much higher than a man.

"What is it?" he asked her.

"Something every Egyptian schoolgirl knows." She smiled mysteriously. "I'll tell you later."

The sun was a great red orb hovering over the steaming jungles of Zaire to the west. The long shadows falling among the rolling foothills below cast the landscape in a wrinkled relief of light and dark. They saw several abandoned mining pits as they followed the chain of mountains that ran along the frontier. Finally Sawyer pointed.

"It's got to be that one up there," he said. There was a deep depression set against the sides of several hills, with a dark semicircular shadow set in the bottom. "Let's fly over for a look-see."

"Uh-uh," Barrabas said. "Too much noise. I don't want them to know I'm coming."

Sawyer nonchalantly reached toward the instrument panel and shut off the little Cessna's engine.

"So we'll glide over quietly. Don't worry. She starts up like that!" He snapped his fingers, grinning broadly.

Sawyer banked the little plane around the eastern edge of the depression, where the sky was darkening into night. Lights and movement were clearly visible at the abandoned copper mine. Barrabas used the pilot's binoculars to study the landscape. He saw the dark square lines of buildings, and men loading cases into two helicopters, but the shadows of evening obscured details.

"Find what you're looking for?"

Barrabas nodded.

"Sure."

"Dead sure."

"That's mighty sure, I guess. Well, there's a grassy plateau we went over a few miles just north of here. I can use it for a landing strip if you really want to go down there.''

For an uncomfortable few moments, restarting the engine was touch and go. It turned and died, turned, died again, and finally, on the third attempt, caught and sputtered to life.

"Told ya!" Sawyer smiled. He banked farther to the east and turned around. The landing on the grassy plateau was rough, but the jolting and bumping, the dangers of an unexpected boulder or dip, didn't deter the intrepid American pilot. When the plane came to a stop, the gray light of evening was fast gathering into night. Barrabas stepped down from the plane. Nara handed him the supplies of food, the AK-47 and the spare ammunition.

Barrabas walked around to the pilot's open window.

"You said your name was Barrabas," Sawyer said. "You got a medal at Quang Doc and a promotion. I think you made colonel. I remember hearing about you now. You pulled a lot of guys through alive."

He sat back, regarding the mercenary for a moment, deep in thought. "You never told me what's here for you."

"A man who has to be stopped before he can do more evil."

"You figure out how you're gonna get out?"

Barrabas shook his head. "I'll deal with that after I finish what I came to do. Then I gotta get Nara to Cairo. I made a promise."

Sawyer slammed his open hand against the instrument panel and then wiped his face. He looked at Barrabas again.

"When I die I know I'll go to heaven..." He recited the lines from Vietnam. "Man, you know something? It's there in your eyes. You're still in hell."

The mercenary turned and walked away from the plane.

"Hey, Barrabas!" Sawyer called to him. Barrabas stopped and faced the pilot.

"Hey, look. Those crates back there. They're full of incendiary bombs. Special shipment for the ANC guerrilla forces in southern Africa. That's what I do, man. After Nam, I stayed in the business. Just like you."

"We do what we do best."

"Yeah. Maybe. Hell, that wasn't my reason. I just didn't want to join the world ever again after Quang Doc. So I ended up here in Africa doing what people paid me to do. Not much of it's up to any good."

Sawyer looked down, considering something. Then he looked at Barrabas again. "You want some help?"

Barrabas started smiling. "I could use a little."

The two men looked at each other, and there was a grim determination in their eyes. They both recognized it. It was the war again.

Sawyer thrust his hand through the window. "Shake, baby. You got it." They ate silently from the supplies in the plane. Afterward, Barrabas and Sawyer went over the plan. They were a mile north of the copper mine. They had to wait another hour for night to settle. Sawyer was to give Barrabas an hour to infiltrate, reconnoiter and take up position. Then he was to fly over, with Nara pushing the small twenty-two-pound bombs from the side door.

The first time around, the incendiary destruction was intended to be diversionary: dropped at the perimeter of the compound where they would do little damage. After that, Sawyer had to play it by ear according to what he saw on the ground.

Nara led Barrabas to a grassy slope out of sight of the airplane and proudly presented him with his new uniform. The black wool fabric of the Bedouin robe had been expertly sewn into loose-fitting pants and a sleeveless jacket. She had fashioned high legged moccasins from the material, inserting the leather soles of the Bedouin sandals into the bottom for protection.

She watched Barrabas dress, silently. As he pulled the jacket on, he felt something hard on the inside. A heavy gold broach with a polished blue stone set in it had been sewn inside the fabric on the spot where his heart was.

"It will protect you from misfortune," Nara explained. She shrugged with a little smile. "A Bedouin good luck charm."

She moved closer. He felt her hand touch his shoulder. He straightened, looking into her dark eyes. She fell against him, and he swept her into his arms, burying his face in her thick dark hair, inhaling the sweet scent of her body. Before he knew what was happening, his lips were pressed against hers, and their tongues played through the warm seal of their mouths.

Barrabas broke away, gasping for breath, feeling her nails dig into his arm as she clung to him.

"Do you . . . ?"

"Yes." She said it without hesitation. "We are husband and wife. That is the purpose of the *mu'tah*."

"I thought it was for protection."

"This, too." She sank in his arms, pulling him to the ground with her arms circling his neck. As they fell, she rolled on top of him. He forced his tongue into her mouth again, wrestling with her lips, her tongue, the sweet, slippery moisture of her mouth, and her tangled hair. His hands moved along the full, graceful curves of her body.

She sat up, opening the long robe and pulling it down over her shoulders. Her breasts were full, her nipples hard, the clean curving lines of her waist and hips gently outlined by the light from the star-filled African sky.

He started to rise so that he could take the jacket off.

"No." Nara pushed him back. "Let me do everything."

Her hands played lightly over his body as she slowly removed his clothes. When they were naked, Barrabas closed his hands around her waist and lifted her from him. He placed her gently on the grassy slope. His mouth met hers again as he entered her, feeling her body quicken, her breath come in gasps as he rose and fell against her firm, smooth body.

For a time—moments, hours, it did not matter—only the struggle of their lovemaking existed. He arched his back and explored her face and neck with his tongue, kissing each breast, his thumbs massaging her taut, hard nipples. Nara's breath caught, and pleasure rippled upward through her body, shaking her. Barrabas thrust forward savagely, feeling his passion surging into her.

They collapsed together in a tangled mass. She looked up at him, her eyes liquid pools of healing water. Barrabas smiled at her, and for the first time in a long time, it seemed, he felt something close to joy.

"That little pyramid in the hills of Burundi...?" Barrabas began, the question springing to mind for no particular reason.

"It marks the southernmost source of the Nile," Nara told him, smiling gleefully.

"There? All the way...it's barely a few miles from here!"

She nodded again and then leaned forward and kissed him, wiping her tongue playfully along his lower lip. A smile of immense happiness was etched across her beautiful face. They said nothing. It was enough that he could not take his eyes off her.

Finally Barrabas rose, putting out his hand to help Nara to her feet.

When they walked back to the airplane, Jack Sawyer glanced at them with a bemused smile. He gave Barrabas a slap on the back.

"About time to get this show started, I'd say."

Barrabas nodded. He smeared his arms with dark wet mud to blacken his skin. Nara handed him a black Bedouin headcloth, and he wrapped it around his head. Only his eyes showed through a crack in the fabric. He tied lengths of stout rope to his belt, and Sawyer gave him a flare gun.

"One green flare and I'll know it's over," he said.

"Good luck," Barrabas told the pilot, shaking his hand.

"To you, too."

Nara stepped forward and kissed Barrabas lightly on the lips. He looked at her face. Her eyes were filled with something he thought he should recognize but refused to name. He held her hand a moment.

"In a while," he said, and turned, his dark figure melting quickly into the African night.

**15**

Two of Banu's soldiers paced slowly in the darkness, their boots clicking on the road outside the open-pit copper mine. One of them occasionally relieved the boredom of long hours on guard duty by kicking at the gravel and sending bits of rock hurtling into the shrub forests lining the road.

They prayed for their duty to be over. They were pulling out in a few hours, leaving their green uniforms and their leader, Banu, and the old mining pit for their homes and families in Ghana, Uganda, Angola, Detroit. Unless the *mzungu* who lived in the great house had more work and more money to pay them to act as his private army somewhere else.

They paused, chatting for a few moments, sharing a joke and then continued to pace.

One of them reached the side of the road and swung around to go back. An arm reached from the shrub, closing like an iron muzzle around his mouth and jerking his head back. The guard grunted in surprise and panic as the razor-sharp knife sliced a great crescent from ear to ear. Blood squirted onto the road.

Hearing the muffled noise, the other guard spun around. Another arm wrapped itself around his neck.

Briefly he felt a dagger jab into his lower back. He
died when it pierced his kidney. He dropped, air es-
caping from his lungs in a long drawn-out burp.
Claude Hayes and Nate Beck stepped into the road.

"Each to his own," Nate murmured, glancing at the
bloody unnatural smile gaping across the neck of the
guard Hayes had taken out. "Yours is messier."

"Yours makes more noise." Hayes lifted the body
by its arms and dragged it into the woods. The two
mercs sank back into the shrubbery and moved closer
to the compound.

They had spent most of the afternoon on top of the
cliffs surrounding the old mine, studying the layout of
the compound and the movement of the guards. There
were several ways down the steep, rocky hillsides to the
rim of the pit. They were debating which route pro-
vided the greatest secrecy when there was a flurry of
movement in the base camp below.

The mercs shuddered with horror when Lee Hatton
and Alex Nanos were dragged from one of the buildings and strung up in the sun. Both looked bruised and
beaten, but they seemed to be conscious, and their will
to fight was evident in the struggle they gave their
captors.

"Think Barrabas is down there, too?" It was a grim
looking Nate Beck who muttered the question.

Hayes shook his head. "Dunno. But I'll tell you one
thing. As of now, our foray tonight is all or nothing.
I say wage a war of attrition. Wait until dark, hit the
road and take out as many of the guards as possible on
the way."

"What if they try something now?"

Hayes pushed his M-16 in front of him. "They're in range. First bastard pulls a gun gets his head blown off."

They took turns watching from the precipice until, toward dusk, the two prisoners were taken down and led back to their prison. Both were on the verge of collapse after hours of dehydration in the hot sun.

"They're all right," Hayes said softly, reassuring Nate. "They got lots left in them. Enough to last until we get there."

But there were unspoken fears at the back of their minds. Was Barrabas already dead? And where was Erika?

Just as the light faded from the western sky, the mercs scrambled down the mountain and slipped into the shrubbery along the road.

They worked their way toward the entrance to the camp, taking out six more guards in pairs along the way. Nate commented that he was getting bored with the monotony. Hayes promised him it would get more exciting.

The routine was broken at the opening of the road where it curved toward the open-pit mine. A branch of the road headed up an incline and ran along the foot of the cliffs to the plateau where the colonial chatêau sat. There were lights and activity in the yard in front of the old house. Green-uniformed men loaded boxes into the helicopter under the supervision of men in long white coats who carried clipboards.

Hayes dispatched his guard easily with his usual method. Nate ran into trouble when he tackled a big brute who, for several moments, survived the toxic shock of an impaled kidney. He broke away from the merc's grasp, his thick arm drawing an enormous machete from his leather belt. Nate lost the grip on his knife and heard a whoosh as the deadly sword sliced through the air. He jumped and rolled, almost feeling the razor-edged steel as it clunked into the road.

Hayes dived from across the road, the knife poised forward in his hand. He drove it into the back of the guard's skull, pushing it through the soft part at the top of the spinal cord until it sank through cartilage and pierced the brain. The guard straightened, his mouth open in a silent scream, and his eyes rolled up to the whites. He collapsed like a puppet whose strings had been cut.

Nate reached for his dagger, which protruded from the dead man's back.

"Forget it! Take this." He handed Nate the machete.

Beck rubbed his thumb over the blade. "Took the edge off when it hit the road," he complained.

"Gimme a break." Hayes laughed and pushed him toward the cliffs.

They climbed to a thin outcropping of rock running for several hundred feet above the road. The mercs dropped down, scrambled over elephant-sized boulders and found a rocky trail that led through a cleft in the rock. It took them behind the château and onto the steep hill that overlooked the rest of the compound. Above, sheer cliffs rose fifty feet. In front of them stood the fuel storage tank, holding thousands of gallons of gasoline.

"I got an idea." Hayes nudged Beck and pointed to the thick plastic fuel lines that led to pumps near the helicopters. "The activity's concentrated on the southern side of the camp, and the building they took Lee and Alex to is on the northern perimeter."

"You mean... Wait!" Nate froze, his gaze directed below. Guards shouted to one another across the compound. Several emerged from one of the buildings, dragging Nanos and Hatton toward the center of the yard. The prisoners struggled and kicked. More guards ran across the compound to assist.

Nate lifted his machete and ran across the rocks to the concrete base that held the storage tank. He struck at the pipe that led down the hill, the blade digging in almost half an inch. He struck again. Gasoline bubbled out and dribbled along the pipe. With the third blow it began to gush.

"Man, I don't know if we have time for this," Hayes told him.

Soldiers were lined up on one side of the yard. They held rifles and stood rigidly at attention, waiting for orders from a big man wearing leopard-skin epaulets. The military formation was unmistakable.

It was a firing squad.

ERIKA WAITED PATIENTLY in the dark, cool room. They brought her food. She couldn't eat. She watched the digital clock on Heiss's desk tick away the minutes to the as yet unspecified hour when she would have one final chance.

Heiss entered with two guards shortly after ten o'clock. He moved awkwardly, turning his shoulders in her direction when he spoke.

"We're ready, Erika." In his hands he held an Uzi submachine gun. "I chose this. You'll find it has very little recoil. There are twenty-six rounds in the mag to ensure you don't miss. And should you have any last-minute ideas about a double-cross, there is a backup firing squad. Their weapons will be aimed at you as well as at the prisoners."

He handed her the automatic weapon. "I'm counting on you."

Erika was ready.

There are points at which tension becomes so palpable, it can be shifted aside like a physical obstruction. Erika had reached that point. She steadied her breathing and followed Heiss down the corridors through the dark old house until they reached the front door.

Straight ahead of her, down the steps and thirty feet across the yard, Lee Hatton and Alex Nanos raised their heads and saw her. Banu shouted an order. Knees high, the line of well-trained soldiers hop-jumped and took up positions along the side of the yard. Banu shouted again. The soldiers raised their rifles to hip level. Heiss leaned his body forward to whisper in her ear.

"Perhaps it would be better a little closer, my dear."

Erika recoiled as his cold, swampy breath fell on her neck.

"Come, my dear," the evil renegade whispered, motioning her to descend the steps, "We don't want you to miss."

BARRABAS LOST PRECIOUS TIME in his descent of the cliffs. Under cover of darkness, he used a rope from Sawyer's airplane to rappel thirty feet down the sheer sides to a ledge that appeared to lead to an incline where a rock face had crumbled to a steep slope. The darkness had deceived him, however. The ledge led to a cul-de-sac, and there was no way to go but back. The danger was, that as time ran out, Sawyer would fly over and drop his incendiary bombs against the cliffs that sheltered him.

He used a second rope, rappelling another fifty feet to the bottom of the mine pit. Lights and the low whine of electric motors on the battery-powered dollies spilled down from the compound. Keeping to the shadows, he circled the immense hole in the ground. The far side rose at a seventy-five-degree angle, but the chiseled rockface afforded grips and holds for his hands and feet.

He climbed to the rim where a patch of darkness fell over the edge. Military commands drifted across the plateau. He pulled himself up the last few feet and scrambled onto his belly on the plateau thirty feet away from the landing pad.

Soldiers and white-coated technicians frantically loaded sealed cardboard boxes aboard two helicopters. In front of the house an execution was being organized. Lee Hatton and Alex Nanos were tied to stakes, their backs to the pit. A line of soldiers ran from the prisoners to the steps. The front door opened.

Barrabas felt a sickening chill. Erika Dykstra stepped out. His worst fear had been realized. Heiss already had her. The svelte, blond woman in soiled khaki slacks and blouse looked nervously around the compound. Heiss stepped from the house, staying close behind her. From the distance, Barrabas could make out the livid white scars along the side of Heiss's head, the way his head appeared to be glued to his shoulder, as if eyes and a mouth had been set on the body of a slug. The merc felt disgust so strong that he could taste it. He spat.

Barrabas glanced at his watch. The big guard with the leopard-skin epaulets shouted an order, and the soldiers jumped, moving their rifles to their hips. There were exactly two minutes to go before the Cessna flew over. Sawyer had promised to turn off the engine and glide again, giving them the double edge— stealth and surprise.

The glow of lights in the compound reached to within a few feet of the pit, giving him darkness to conceal his movement. He ran along the rim until he came up almost behind the execution posts. The imprisoned mercs awaited their deaths less than twenty feet from him.

Barrabas took in the scene with growing horror. Erika descended the steps, holding a small submachine gun in front of her. The renegade CIA agent stood ten feet behind her. His mouth moved, speaking to her, smiling cruelly. She aimed the rifle at the doomed captives. In the insane world ruled by Karl Heiss, Erika Dykstra was the executioner.

Banu shouted an order.

The soldiers raised their rifles to their shoulders. Heiss spoke sharply.

The fireworks were about to begin.

Barrabas could wait no longer.

WITH HEISS'S TAUNTING VOICE taunting, coaxing, Erika raised the Uzi. The humming incandescent lights on overhead poles cast an eerie yellow glow over the compound that ended abrubtly at the hard edge of the impenetrable African night.

Banu shouted. Sweat glistened on the black faces of the soldiers. They raised their rifles to their shoulders and aimed. No one seemed to notice the dark puddle trickle across the yard almost under their boots. Twenty feet in front of her, Lee Hatton and Alex Nanos lifted their heads and looked at Erika.

If one of them said something, the Dutch woman didn't hear it. The world had become silent. It was time now. She had failed in part, but she could do the rest—kill the man who had murdered the person she loved more than anything in the world: Nile Barrabas.

She spun sideways, knuckles white on the Uzi in front of her. As she squeezed the trigger, she screamed with the rage of a treed jungle cat.

"I loved him! I loved Barrabas more than anyone who ever lived! I came to kill you, Heiss! *You*! It was you who tried to kill my brother. I want you to die!"

The Uzi failed to fire. Karl Heiss stared at her, his face lit with excitement. He started to laugh, his body bent back, welded to his twisted face. The soldiers snickered. The gun was a dud.

Heiss reached a hand inside his jacket and pulled out a pistol. He leveled his eyes at her.

"Now *I* . . . will kill *you*."

"No, Heiss!"

The shout came from the darkness past the execution stakes. Suddenly a man in black burst into the pool of light, aiming an automatic rifle at the former CIA agent. He tore off the cloth binding his head. His hair was white, and his eyes flashed like blue ice. There was no mercy in them for the master of evil.

Heiss's mouth opened and issued a scream from the fanged red slit. It was an order to fire.

A sound like a blanket flapping in a heavy wind grew from the hillside.

Just what he ordered.

A wall of flame burst from the ground in front of Banu and his soldiers. The men screamed, jumping back from the fire. Their uniforms caught fire, and they ran, fleeing flames from which there was no escape. An explosion shook the compound. A sheet of chemical fire licked up the sides of the cliffs, bathing the buildings with the bluish-white light of superhot incendiary bombs.

Barrabas fired, too.

Heiss's neckless face disappeared as the heavy Kalashnikov lead opened crimson splotches in his head. The impact of the bullets lifted him from his shoes, spun him in the air and tossed him like a bag of garbage onto the steps of the house.

Suddenly two men ran full tilt around the corner of the old house, familiar faces in a time of need. Claude Hayes and Nate Beck saluted Barrabas with upraised autorifles.

"Colonel, we gotta move—" Hayes shouted. His words were cut off by a fiery convulsion that shook the valley. On the hillside above the old house, a column of flame sixty feet high spewed above the cliffs, hurling the fuel storage tank over the compound in a rain of red-hot metal. The roof of the old house caught, and in seconds the upper story was a raging inferno.

There was rifle fire, and bullets joined the haze of death. The soldiers by the helicopters were shooting back. The scientists dropped their clipboards and jumped aboard the choppers. Pilots frantically revved the engines, and rotors turned, fanning the flames spreading across the yard to the cardboard crates.

Barrabas, Hayes and Beck swung around and returned a scathing line of autofire. Soldiers spun, jerked, danced and fell. Others made it to the helicopters and tried to jump aboard. More hostile fire came in scattered bursts from cover of the dollies.

Suddenly, like a giant bat swooping out of darkness, Sawyer's Cessna glided over the pit. A dark object plummeted from the cargo door. The choppers were consumed in an immense golden sun of chemical flames. Fire raged from the stone house, and the upper stories collapsed into the interior, sending a pillar of sparks and burning debris high into the night sky.

Barrabas felt the heat flickering across his face.

"I'll help Nate," Hayes said, heading past him. Beck was already untying the two mercs bound to the stakes.

Barrabas jerked the flare gun from his belt. He held his arm over his head. Victory. He pulled the trigger, and the brilliant green light fired into the air like a roman candle.

Erika stood in the center of the compound, frozen. He walked across the yard toward her, his heart pounding in his chest. Her face was stained with tears, and she shivered like a kitten pulled from an icy well.

She saw him approach, his familiar face blocking out the jungles of hell. When he stood before her, she looked at him, her blue eyes lost and alone. She pointed to the spot where Heiss had been hit. Blood stained the ground. A pair of shoes lay on the dirt. No more.

The front of the house had crumpled, entombing Heiss's body in a pile of rock ten feet deep.

"Where . . . "

Erika reacted with barely a shrug. The color drained from her face. Barrabas put out his arms and she collapsed into them, sobbing. He held her for a long, long time.

THE DAUGHTER OF THE NILE, Cairo, spread through the yellow desert haze, the din of human traffic seething through in the maze of her frantic streets.

Barrabas stood beside Nara on the terrace outside the University Hospital. He watched the winds blowing in from the Western Desert stir the brilliant flowers neatly planted along the wall, waiting for his last moments with his Bedouin wife to end.

Nara was dressed in Western clothing, the white skirt and pale blouse setting off her dark skin and black hair.

"I can't understand why the Bedouins would want to cover their women, if they're all as beautiful as you," Barrabas mused.

Nara laughed. "There is a certain attraction to the mysterious. But I think I shall enjoy my return to modern life."

They were silent a few minutes. A taxi pulled slowly to the curb below the wall. Barrabas raised a hand to hail it.

"What now?"

"I will work for the Egyptian government, in the agency that deals with nomadic people. The Bedouins."

"And the *mu'tah*?"

"It ended automatically. The moment we arrived in Cairo yesterday. Are you sad?"

Three days had passed since the Zairian holocaust.

Government soldiers had arrived several hours after the conflagration had destroyed much of Heiss's compound. There had been no prisoners. The few remaining soldiers in the private army had quickly fled into the mountains. The mercs, Erika, Nara and Jack Sawyer had been kept under heavy guard for twelve hours while word of what had happened had been sent via Kinshasa to Washington and New York. With Jessup's intervention, they had been released. Sawyer had flown them to Cairo. This time he had said he would write it off as a promotion when Barrabas tried to arrange payment.

On the way, not far from the Zairian-Burundi border, they had landed on a gravel road and walked to the top of a hill where the small pyramid stood shoulder high and cold, clear water gurgled from a fissure in the rocks, marking the humble source of the Nile.

Nara had brought him a cup of the liquid. After Barrabas had drunk it, she had repeated words of wisdom that dated from the days before the Pyramids had been built.

"He who drinks from the Nile returns to drink again."

Now, on the terrace outside the Cairo hospital, Barrabas repeated it to her, smiling easily.

"Goodbye," she said, touching his hand.

"The *mu'tah*. It was a good bargain."

"The best."

Nara kissed him lightly and turned toward the taxi. Barrabas watched until it pulled away. Almost immediately, a second taxi slowed to a stop. Nate Beck and Alex Nanos hopped from the back. Lee Hatton left the front seat.

Nanos reached his arm back inside. Out stepped a belly dancer, a voluptuous Arab beauty with Rubensesque thighs and a diaphanous green harem suit.

"I see you're already back in top form," Barrabas said, laughing as his soldiers climbed the steps.

Nanos shot him an eager smile. "Colonel, I'm sore all over. But Azila here's a present for Gunter."

"He's barely out of his coma, he can't talk, has total amnesia, and you bring him a dancing girl?"

"A man's got priorities, Colonel," Nate joked.

"Seriously, Colonel," Alex explained. "The doctors say he'll regain his memory faster if he has familiar things around him. Know what I mean?" The Greek winked.

"You gotta hand it to Alex for trying," Lee Hatton said to Barrabas. She stood beside the colonel, watching Nanos and Beck lead the maiden past the wide-eyed security guards at the hospital entrance.

"How about you, Lee? Alex is obviously back to normal. Are you okay?"

"We weren't fed or watered very well. Just enough to keep us alive through those afternoons in the sun. I clocked every microsecond. Never has time moved more slowly."

"Tell me about it." Barrabas meant it ironically, his own memory of the desert still daunting.

"But other than that and a few bruises we're both okay. What I'd like to know is what was really going on in that secret laboratory in the Zairian mountains."

"What do you mean?"

Lee narrowed her eyes, puffed up her cheeks in concentration and considered her words. "I didn't get to see much because the government troops got there and rounded us up. But in the time we had to look around I saw the equipment in some of those buildings. There was weird stuff going on." She paused, finding it difficult to proceed.

"I'm listening," Barrabas urged.

"Well, I'm a medical doctor, not a researcher, so I'm no expert, Colonel. But I've seen genetics labs.

And I've seen biological and germ-warfare labs. Heiss had the equipment there, and presumably the expertise to use it. He had to have backers—for money, secrecy, for a network to recruit from.''

"And the Zairian government has thrown the wraps around everything. We might never know.''

Lee nodded. "Guess it'll pay to keep our eyes open from now on. Coming in?'' She gestured toward the hospital.

Barrabas shook his head, his eyes clouded over with troubling thoughts. "I'm waiting for Erika. There she is now.''

The Dutch woman hurried through the front doors of the hospital, waving to Lee as the two women passed. She reached out her hand and took Barrabas's when she came to his side.

"Gunter's going to be fine,'' she told him. "It'll take months of rehabilitation and some plastic surgery. But he'll be fine.''

"Especially with Alex and Nate working on the therapy.''

Erika laughed. "I saw her on the way up. All two hundred pounds. I shouldn't be catty. Gunter likes big women.''

She drew close to Barrabas, noticing from his expression that his thoughts had drifted away again, gone to the place to which only soldiers went, a city of war into which she could never follow him. This time, she vowed, she would not to be afraid of it.

"What are you thinking?'' Barrabas asked her.

"That Heiss has done enough to us, that if we don't work it out somehow, we're fools. We'd be letting him win."

Barrabas put his strong arm around her shoulders.

"I'm glad he's dead," she said, leaning into him.

Barrabas flinched, then braced himself, debating what should be said, what was best avoided. Karl Heiss was only the tip of a monstrous iceberg. Killing him was as effective as exterminating a single cockroach. And after the tumult of battle and fire that had raged across the compound, Barrabas had not actually seen the body. Heiss had been buried under the collapsed wall of the stone house. Now the soldiers had the corpse. If there was one.

"So am I," he said, shouldering the burden of inconclusiveness behind the simple words.

# 4 FREE BOOKS
# 1 FREE GIFT
## NO RISK
## NO OBLIGATION
# NO KIDDING

# TAKE 'EM NOW

## FOLDING SUNGLASSES FROM GOLD EAGLE

Mean up your act with these tough, street-smart shades. Practical, too, because they fold 3 times into a handy, zip-up polyurethane pouch that fits neatly into your pocket. Rugged metal frame. Scratch-resistant acrylic lenses. Best of all, they can be yours for only $6.99. **MAIL ORDER TODAY.**

Send your name, address, and zip code, along with a check or money order for just $6.99 + .75¢ for postage and handling (for a total of $7.74) payable to Gold Eagle Reader Service, a division of Worldwide Library. New York and Arizona residents please add applicable sales tax.

Remove from pouch...

unfold once...

unfold twice...

and they're ready to wear.

**GOLD EAGLE**

Gold Eagle Reader Service
901 Fuhrmann Blvd.
P.O. Box 1325
Buffalo, N.Y. 14240-1325

*Offer not available in Canada.*

GFS1-RRR